JOE HOWE'S GHOST

BRETTON LONEY

BRETTON LONEY

JOE HOWE'S GHOST

JOE HOWE'S GHOST

Erin Curran is a rookie Government MLA when a startling encounter with the ghost of Joe Howe, Nova Scotia's most famous politician and journalist, changes the trajectory of her career and her life.

Howe has been silently walking the halls of historic Province House for more than 150 years and Erin is the first living soul he has spoken to in all that time.

At first, it is Erin who learns from Howe, the master politician and communicator, who brought responsible government to Nova Scotia, defended free speech and bitterly opposed Confederation.

But as their friendship grows, Howe gains an appreciation of our times as Erin faces the trials of today's politics and the unique challenges facing female MLAs—from sexist colleagues to misogynist social media trolls.

Joe Howe's Ghost is a reflection on Howe's tumultuous political era and of provincial politics today, and an exploration of the personal struggle between the desire for political power and upholding heartfelt personal convictions that are common to both.

Joe Howe's Ghost

Bretton Loney

ISBN 978-1-7753933-2-0

Cover design by Ivan Zanchetta

Discover other titles by Bretton Loney at
www.brettonloney.com

DEDICATION

To Darrel Thorson and to the late Doug Forsyth, good friends I debated politics with for decades, not always agreeing, but relishing the discussion.

To my colleagues in newsrooms in Newfoundland and Nova Scotia, and in the Government of Nova Scotia and the Alberta Legislature, who taught me so much about politics, democracy, and the important role that an informed media plays in both.

To my parents, Jeanette and the late Roy Loney, who nourished my interest in current affairs at our kitchen table and taught me to speak my mind, and to my brothers, Todd and Troy, who have kept those family traditions alive.

To my children, Kier and Cale, their partners Kirk and Amy, who try to keep me current and to my grandchildren, Jonis and Jorah, who make the future magical.

Finally, to my wife, Karen Shewbridge, who has listened to me go on and on about politics for nearly 40 years and has engaged me in a continuous and challenging conversation which I hope never ends.

CHAPTER 1

The second time I saw him I felt him first. Every hair tingled. The taste of metal coated my tongue. The speaker piping in the drone of late-night debate from my fellow MLAs fell silent. I was alone in the Legislative Library, and it was as still as a tomb.

At the top of the winding, wrought iron staircase to the second-floor book stacks was a shape. To the left of a portrait of the Duke of Kent. No more than a shadow in a room cloaked in semi-darkness. I shook my head. After a sleepless night pacing the floor with a sick toddler in my arms, I was too exhausted to be at work.

In the gloom a hand formed grasping the railing so tightly a row of knuckles popped up. An elderly man took shape out of the nothingness. He had a large head, a wild crown of white hair, and a turnip-shaped nose.

He wore a long, dark frock coat with a white, high-collared shirt, a vest, and a bow tie. His left hand was hooked on the lapel of the frock coat. His feet anchored as though steadying himself on a rocking ship. He gazed down on me from under winged eyebrows.

"Good evening, madam," he said formally, his voice hoarse and dusty as though unused for a long time.

Eight porcelain busts mounted along the walls turned their heads toward him ever so slightly.

The freakish movement was startling. Winded me like a punch to the stomach. I blurted out "Good evening" as my head fell to the table and the world went black.

~

"JOE, you sh-sh-sh-should not have appeared out of the blue like that. You s-s-scared the young woman nearly out of her wits. She has fainted straight away."

"For goodness sake, Ennis, I know. I couldn't help myself. Over the years we have crept around here, I have tried to reach out to many of these fellows. To dissuade them from poor policies or to encourage certain bills, but I could never make a connection. Then, the first time I try with this young woman, something magical happens. I feel as though I have been struck by a thunderbolt."

"She does remind one of your lovely wife, does she not?"

"Of my own little editor, my dearest Susie? Do you think so?"

"You know that she does. Her spirit and intelligence shine through in this p-p-place, not to mention the adorable little nose and those hazel eyes. It's quite remarkable."

"God's teeth, that is it exactly. I have seen her dozens of times in these hallways. Her keen mind and grace are evident whether she is conversing with members of her own party or fellows from the other side of the House. She listens carefully and politely, weighing their words, never offering too much nor too little of her own opinion until she has the perfect thing to say. Rather extraordinary."

"Our Nova Scotia needs someone like her, Joe, more than ever."

"I feel awful for scaring her. Quite diabolical of me. Should I try to revive her? Blow in her face or tap on the table beside her head?"

"I think you have done quite enough for one night. It has been nearly 150 years since you last conversed with the living. I think you can give the young woman a day or two to try and understand what she has seen before attempting again. I am sure you have plenty to say to her, but it can wait. I have tried to be good company for you since I came over, Joe, but admittedly I have not been as good a conversationalist, and as good a listener, as I was at first. One grows tired."

"My friend, you have been fine company. It is I who have grown tedious. I am tired of this place, the unchanging nature of the issues and, most of all, of politicians. I long for eternal sleep, but somehow you and I seem impervious to its charms. For some reason known only to fate, I have made a tenuous connection with this promising young woman, and I must say it fills me with hope. We should raise a bumper of wine in celebration, but of course that is not possible. Yes, we will let her sleep and gather her thoughts. I must be a fright to the living, eh, Ennis?"

"And to the dead too, s-s-s-speaking on behalf of the dearly departed."

CHAPTER 2

"This thing is ruining us, Premier. It's causing trouble, plenty of it. I heard about it the moment I walked into Tim Hortons back home. Something needs to be done, that's all I'm saying."

With that Gerry Johnson sits down, flushed and sweating, the seventh or eighth of my caucus colleagues to speak to our latest political scandal. Some eloquently, others passionately, while a few couldn't marshal a coherent sentence, let alone a rational argument. There's more than thirty of us packed into the caucus office boardroom on this surprisingly hot, early October day, and the heating system is already in winter mode, so it's a sauna.

It has been the wildest caucus meeting since I was elected a year ago. Almost out of control. Since the scandal broke last week, our party has been under attack in the traditional media and on social. People on Facebook, newspaper columnists, editorials, and callers to radio talk shows are angrily urging the premier to kick Duncan McDonald out of cabinet.

The party is bleeding support, yet for some reason the

premier, normally a savvy politician, is sticking with McDonald. Dunc, as everyone calls him, is a toady of a man who's everything that's wrong about Nova Scotia politics. A professional politician with twenty years at the provincial level and ten as a county councillor, he owned a small-town tire shop before getting into the game. His cabinet post is the best-paying job he's ever had or ever will.

He's uneducated, unsophisticated, and untravelled, unless you count his five trips to Las Vegas, which he goes on and on about. He doesn't understand most of the issues facing his department yet blows off briefings with staff because he knows better. I'm not certain he can actually read. What keeps getting Dunc elected is he seems to be everybody's friend. Smiling, joking, backslapping, the works. He knows every family in his district and the names of all the staff and security guards in the Legislature, but he's shady.

"And how's our Erin Curran doing?" he had said on the way into the meeting, a leering grin creeping out from under his unkempt beard as he adjusted the belt well hidden under his pot belly. "Nice to see ya again. People are sayin' good things about ya. The party needs pretty, smart young women like yourself."

Our caucus, even some of Dunc's cabinet colleagues, realizes we need to cut this dead weight loose, still the premier is standing by his man for God knows what reason. Loyalty to an old party soldier? Some misguided hope this will all blow over? Or does Dunc have something on the premier? They go way back.

I'm still shaken by what happened last night in the library, but for now it's taken a back seat to what's going on in this sweltering boardroom.

"Look, nothing personal, Dunc, but this isn't going away,

if anything it's getting bigger," says Doug Brayfield, a city MLA like me and a friend. "Premier, it's a media feeding frenzy, and something needs to be done to take the air out of it."

Doug leaves it at that. We've chatted and both think Dunc should be tossed from cabinet. It blows my mind that smart, hard-working MLAs like Doug and our colleague Nathalie Amirault who got into politics for the right reasons sit on the backbenches while dinosaurs like Dunc roam the frontbenches as cabinet ministers.

"Doug, I appreciate your concern, I appreciate all your concerns," says the premier. "Look, I've been in the game for a long time, and I know we can ride this out. Bob and Janet can tell you it's not any different than the Larkin scandal eleven years ago, the last time we formed government," he says, glancing over at two of our longest-serving cabinet ministers. "We weathered that one and we'll weather this one. Dunc is doing a great job. He's served this province, his constituents, and our party well. I'm showing him the same respect and loyalty that I would show any of you. Remember that."

The premier pointedly makes eye contact with everyone at the table to drive his last point home.

"Premier, this scandal is affecting the way people think of our Government, the way they think about all of us. We're going to take a big hit in the polls."

The normally easygoing premier gives Doug a look that makes it clear discussion is over.

"I think it's time to move to our next agenda item, folks. What's next?"

The caucus chair hesitates for an extra second before falling in line and moving on to the next item despite the grim faces and tense body language. I thought the premier might be losing control, but he hasn't yet.

I'm continually astounded by how much party politics is like a wolf pack. Everyone eventually falls in line with the Alpha—and in Nova Scotia it's always a male—to move up in status. If you don't, you'll never get into cabinet. You get so frozen out of power and influence that you either quit or are forced out. Religious shunning has nothing on what political parties do to members who buck the system.

As the meeting breaks up, the room is buzzing like an angry wasp's nest. My colleagues are upset. Some don't like Dunc, some are embarrassed by his latest screw-up, and others worry about being dragged down to electoral defeat by this fiasco. Their reputations as well as MLA and cabinet salaries are on the line. But they have to be careful. To stand up to the premier, or even old Dunc, is dangerous. Dunc is the kind of infighter who, the first chance he gets, will shank anyone in the back who spoke against him. And Dunc never forgets.

"This is fucking stupid," Doug whispers as we walk out of the room, Dunc and the premier standing nearby, smiling and shaking hands—a greying wolf paying homage to the pack leader. Dunc might as well kiss his ass.

CHAPTER 3

I'm trying to figure out what happened. I was a zombie after pacing the floors the night before with Zoey. She wouldn't go to Robbie, so I didn't get a break. It wasn't the first time in the middle of the night that I've regretted that great, unprotected tent sex at Kejimkujik Park. Of course, the next morning when I see Zoey's innocent face at the breakfast table I feel guilty for such thoughts.

I would chalk up what I saw to sleep deprivation if it wasn't the second time it's happened. One afternoon a couple of weeks ago, I was alone in the Veterans Room, a beautiful meeting space on the main floor of Province House, when I saw a shape in a corner of the room, next to the fireplace. It looked like an old man had stepped out of a nineteenth-century painting. Then he was gone. It was freaky. I couldn't figure out what it was. A reflection in a mirror from one of the dozens of portraits of grumpy, old men that hang on every wall of the place? An odd shadow cast by the setting sun? It was there and then gone in the midst of a hectic day, so I tried to forget about it.

Last night's presence, the same man, lasted more than a

few seconds and talked to me. Well, said a couple of words before I crumpled like a used paper cup. I've never fainted, but I was glad I did. I couldn't process what I saw and heard. It wasn't rational.

"Erin, don't forget you've got that thing at the Canada Games Centre at seven," says Nada, my constituency assistant, as she walks in and sees me staring blankly out my office window at the charming view of the strip mall parking lot below.

"The soccer thing or the immigrant association thing?"

"The soccer thing. The immigration event is tomorrow night, remember? Okay, I'm off to the daycare to pick up the kid."

I don't know what I'd do without Nada Nesrallah. A steady stream of constituency cases, speaking requests, and party information flows in and out of this office every day, and somehow she keeps on top of it all.

I didn't tell Robbie the first time I saw the ghost, and I didn't tell him about this one either. I can't exactly say why. My husband is a good man, obsessed with politics and becoming a partner at his law firm, but he's a loving spouse and great with Zoey. I guess I didn't tell him because he's not good at understanding anything you can't capture on your phone or plot on a spreadsheet. He has no time for alternative medicine or anything you can't quantify. He finds some of my friends a bit much, especially Summer and her latest hipster girlfriend. If I don't have a photo or five seconds of video of what I think I saw, I better keep quiet. If I tell Robbie, he'll send me to a specialist for a CT scan and start worrying about a brain aneurism or a cyst. Still, I might check in with our GP for a quick physical.

I've got to figure out what happened before I say anything to Robbie. I don't believe in ghosts, and I've never had a paranormal experience. Friends have. Summer swears she saw the ghost of Anna Leonowens years ago when she was studying at the College of Art and Design. I never thought much about it. It was Summer and she's a bit dramatic. Besides, she was probably high.

I'm not on any meds, haven't smoked weed in months, and hardly manage to gulp down more than a glass of Pinot Grigio at night before I fall asleep, exhausted from either Zoey or my crazy new career in politics.

I need to get away to Mom and Dad's cottage for a few days by myself to process what happened last night. It's not every day that a spirit who looks like one of the most famous Nova Scotians in history wishes you good evening. But between my busy schedule with the Legislature in session, Robbie's sixty-hour weeks, and Zoey the energy vampire, a trip to the cottage isn't happening any time soon.

CHAPTER 4

The Dunc McDonald hurricane is starting to blow itself out, although it isn't calm yet. The Opposition continues to ask questions in the Legislature, but media coverage is slimmer and the story no longer leads newscasts. Reporters are getting bored without any new revelations to feed the story. The Government and party's social media accounts are full of the vilest stuff, and Government MLAs, including me, are getting angry calls, emails, and tweets from constituents. I can't escape Hurricane Dunc at home either. Robbie worked for our party as an executive assistant to two cabinet ministers before joining a law firm, so he can't stop obsessing about it.

"It's this kind of shit that kills a government," Robbie has repeated in a hundred different ways, at the breakfast table, in midday texts, and before we turn out the lights. "We might as well not have bothered with all the good legislation and programs we've brought in, because all anyone will remember is what that asshole did."

I swear he even muttered something about it under his breath when we were in the middle of sex the other night. I stopped what we were doing for a minute, and he was so turned on he never said another word.

I couldn't even get away from it when I got together with Summer at our favourite North End Halifax bistro. Politics never comes up when we're hanging out. She's one of my oldest friends. We go way back to Fairview Junior High and were inseparable during high school at Halifax West. No one could figure out what we had in common then, and no one can now, especially Robbie, who finds her partial buzz-cut, multiple piercings, and tattoos a bit much.

"This Dunc guy is a dick," Summer said, as she munched on roasted Brussels sprouts. "We paid for that dick to go to Las Vegas four times in one year. Four times, Curran. He blew enough money to cover a year's worth of funding for an artist's co-op."

"It was five times in fifteen months, and it was for conferences to do with his job as Minister of Gaming and Lotteries, one of his two cabinet posts. But yeah, you're right, he's a dick."

I left it at that because the more you get into the details, the worse it gets. Of course, Las Vegas hosts loads of gambling conferences. The Nova Scotia minister responsible has been going to one of the biggest industry conferences in Vegas annually for years, but only one per year.

Dunc loved his first conference and the post-conference activities so much that his deputy minister had to drag him home a couple of days after it was over. Dunc then booked himself into four more Vegas gambling conferences in the span of a year. The premier prides himself on running a tight ship when it comes to travel spending. Ministers don't travel a lot and don't take many departmental staff when they go to conferences or federal–provincial meetings, but at least one or two are normally there to advise them.

Dunc stopped bringing staff with him. He also rang up some big-ticket hotel and expense bills, arriving at the conventions early and leaving late. He spent about twenty-five days in Vegas at about $700 a day for hotels and meals, plus airfare and conference fees, according to media reports. It added up to a bill of nearly $40,000, and taxpayers aren't happy.

Government tried to shrug it off, saying that Dunc was new to the department and needed to get up to speed about a complicated industry. Fortunately for us, the latest quarterly report on provincial gambling revenues showed a slight uptick, which we attributed to Dunc's careful and informed management. Yeah, Summer and Robbie are right, Dunc is a dick.

The controversy hasn't made the fall sitting any easier. It riled up the Official Opposition, making it difficult to get them to cooperate with us on anything, let alone moving various bills through the legislative process. So here we are again with another night sitting.

Unlike my fellow MLAs, who drink coffee in the members' lounge just outside the legislative chamber during breaks or duck outside for a quick smoke, I like to relax in the quiet of the Legislative Library. The room is something out of a Jane Austen novel. The kind of library Lord Broodingly Handsome would have had in his manor house. Inside you're surrounded by thousands of books, books, and more books, even on the wall that's dominated by a six-foot-high, Palladian-arched window overlooking Hollis Street.

I sit alone at one of the wooden, leather-inlaid reading tables, near busts of a young Queen Victoria and her husband, Prince Albert. At one end of the library hangs a portrait of Malachai Salter, a member of the first legislative assembly in 1758. At the other, a portrait of Prince Edward, Duke of Kent and Strathearn, Victoria's father, but best known locally for constructing Halifax's Town Clock and the Prince's Lodge on Bedford Basin.

I've only been sitting here for a few minutes when that same copper taste creeps onto my tongue. The hairs on my body quiver like the finely tuned antennae of an insect. I look over my shoulder and there he stands—shimmering like a hologram before gaining form, his face white as printer paper—as he first stood on the floor of Province House more than 180 years ago or on stages in halls and barns across Nova Scotia, firing people's hearts and minds with his words. For there is no doubt who this pale, elderly figure resembles.

"Good evening, madam. I am indeed sorry for the fright I must have given you when we last met. My humblest apologies. Regretfully, I did not have the opportunity to introduce myself. Joe Howe at your service," he says, bowing his old, white head.

He stands in his frock coat at the top of one of the two wrought iron staircases that twist their way to the second-floor bookshelves, which are protected by iron railings trimmed with intertwined mayflowers. I shake myself, hoping he will disappear, but nothing changes.

"Of course, I know who you are, Mr. Howe. Everyone in Nova Scotia knows your name. I feel crazy saying this, but good evening, Mr. Howe. I'm Erin Curran."

"It is a pleasure to be formally introduced, Mrs. Curran. I hope you do not mind me calling you by your Christian name, Erin. I am not one for formalities. Some suggest I am too familiar, but I hope that is not the case," he says, before slowing descending the stairs. "The sight of you is a delight to these sad, old eyes."

"I'm hardly delightful looking, Mr. Howe, especially after the day I've had."

"Please, it is simply Joe."

I've never been overly vain about my looks. I'm attractive enough when dressed up, blessed by Mom's slim figure but not her curly hair, having inherited Dad's thick brown mop instead. I have a small scar above my left eyebrow from a childhood incident with a swing that concealer can hide most days. Everyone says I have Mom's button nose, whatever that means, and Dad's angular jaw.

"I understand that your governing party had a difficult week with the public and from my former colleagues in the newspapers over a scandal involving Mr. McDonald. These political travails can be extraordinarily challenging, nonetheless they build character in one and one's colleagues. Trust me on this."

His voice is not much more than a whisper, yet the words are clear and precise. Joe Howe, that Joe, discussing the politics of the day with me.

"This matter seems most unfortunate, though. I recognize as a party man that one feels obliged to support one's colleagues through thick and thin. Even so, Mr. McDonald's actions in this matter are simply indefensible. I have always found this kind of skullduggery beyond contempt, no less so in your time than in mine. It is, after all, not his money that has been spent. Rather, it is that of our fellow Nova Scotians who have provided it to the provincial treasury through their hard-earned labours."

He sighs from the depths of himself.

"Sometimes I wonder if we did the right thing adopting party politics in our beloved Nova Scotia. During my long years of purgatory here in this House, I have come to regret it. I have seen that it makes it impossible to pull the bad weeds from the flower garden."

Joe's manner is so friendly and unthreatening that in spite of his being a ghost and about the most famous man in Nova Scotia in history, it feels like I'm chatting with my favourite elderly uncle or with a neighbour. "I agree, Dunc's actions are way out of line. All we've done for the past few weeks is defend him. Some of my colleagues and I think he should be thrown out of cabinet. Sadly, I don't think that's going to happen."

"It is a regretful and unfortunate state of affairs. I apologize, Erin, I must leave you. This brief but delightful discussion on politics has exhausted me. Conversation with the living is new to me and apparently rather draining. I do not have the vitality I once had. Be that as it may, it has been my pleasure. I look forward to our next conversation."

With that, Joe Howe starts to shimmer and dissolves into the air, taking my previous concept of reality with him.

CHAPTER 5

ada has gone home for the evening, and I've got another couple of hours to go until I can join Robbie and Zoey for a late supper. I have more constituency cases to slog through to figure out how I can navigate the labyrinth of government programs to make things happen for people. The glamorous Friday nights of a provincial politician, or at least this one.

I put some music on my laptop, and the empty office is flooded by NSYNC's "Bye, Bye, Bye." I keep this guilty pleasure hidden from most people, especially Summer and Robbie, who roll their eyes at my undying love for this boy band. It's been days since I last saw Joe, and I'm trying to process it. I'm pretty sure I didn't have some kind of psychotic episode. I'm not talking to anyone else who is dead. I haven't had any recent emotional losses or trauma. I haven't been struck on the head, and I'm healthy, although exhausted.

Having said that, all my thirtysomething friends with careers and kids are the same. We all complain about the lack of time for romance, dining out, or good sex. Who has the energy for that now? Most of my friends would choose a good night's sleep over sex. Or time to get together with girl-friends to chat and laugh over some wine.

I should be settling back to my work, but instead I'm thinking about Joe. After my encounter with him, I've come to realize how little I know about the man. Like every Nova Scotia kid, I know he was a famous provincial politician and journalist. I remember he won a famous libel trial and represented himself. That he was a well-respected editor and publisher of the *Novascotian* newspaper.

I LEARNED some of Joe's history in the newspaper business from Dad, who was a long-time copy editor at the *Halifax Chronicle*. Dad thinks Joe Howe is the greatest Nova Scotian ever. He doesn't understand why Howe isn't as recognized in Canadian history books as other nineteenth-century jour-nalists-turned-political-reformers like Ontario's William Lyon Mackenzie and George Brown or the exotically named Amor de Cosmos of British Columbia.

Dad is always after me to read books about Joe that he's collected, and I've tried to read a few. But while I followed Dad into the newspaper business, at least for a few years, I never inherited his passion for Joe or that era of Nova Scotia history. I couldn't see the relevance of Joe Howe and his white, anglophile contemporaries to today's province and politics.

I remember that Joe had something to do with Nova Scotia achieving "responsible government," not that I could tell you what responsible government means. I also know that he fought against Nova Scotia joining Confederation in

1867 but was eventually won over and joined Sir John A. Macdonald's federal cabinet.

That's the sum total of what I know about my dad's hero. A degree in political science from Dalhousie, a bachelor of journalism from the University of King's College, and time in the provincial media, yet I know squat about the guy whose statue has stood next to Province House for more than a hundred years. Pathetic.

It reminds me of my days as a young reporter, sent out to cover people and events I had absolutely no context for and being expected to return with an interesting story for the *Chronicle*'s readers that made some kind of sense. I was always more successful if I did as much research as I could before my interviews. That's it. I need to prepare for any future encounters with Joe as though they're interviews that any journalist or historian would kill to have. And to do that, I need to know more than I do.

When we go to Mom and Dad's for Sunday dinner I'll borrow some of Dad's books. Mom will assume I'm humouring Dad in his old age. Robbie won't know what's up, as he's the guy with the one-thousand-page biographies of Churchill and Kennedy on his night table, and I'm the one with the latest life-affirming, Oprah-endorsed novel piled by the bed, or a book of poetry.

I close my laptop and head home to my family.

CHAPTER 6

"Joe, I saw the premier and Mr. McDonald walking toward the Veterans Room, and they look rather s-s-serious. You might want to rouse yourself from that chair and see what foolishness they may be up to."

"Oh, very well, Ennis. I am sure it is your typical political nonsense, nonetheless you are right that it might prove interesting, or at least insightful. I once had hopes for our premier, yet he has disappointed me to such a large extent I find I hardly bother to listen anymore."

"Gather yourself. You do not move as quickly as you once did. If you dillydally much longer there will have been no point in you going there for a listen."

~

"So that's it, Dunc, it's not looking good for old Bob. He's got another round of tests with his specialist, but it's definitely cancer again. After the last time, he told me the odds of surviving another round weren't great. Getting diagnosed with cancer three times in ten years is never good."

"That's terrible. He's always been a good soldier for the party. It ain't easy to replace an old warhorse like Bob, if that's what's needed. You know, until he gets his health back."

"Dunc, we've both been around the block. If Bob has to step down on account of this, he won't be coming back. That's why I need your thoughts on his replacement. It won't happen today or tomorrow, but we'll need to be ready to pull the trigger in the next couple of weeks. Of course, I've talked to the party president and we've batted it around on the seventh floor. LeBlanc has some thoughts on it, and you probably know what her gut instinct is."

"I'm sure I do. Instead of doing the smart thing and replacing Bob with another Valley MLA, your chief of staff will want some cappuccino-swillin' Halifax MLA. Hell, Premier, we're the party of rural Nova Scotia. We only need to win a handful of seats in Halifax. So long as we sweep the rural mainland and split Cape Breton fifty-fifty with the Official Opposition, we're in."

"The numbers aren't looking good, Dunc. We're only eighteen months out from an election. We need to pick up some seats in Halifax-Dartmouth. We're going to put some more focus on city issues. LeBlanc is right. We need another city cabinet minister. So, who's it going to be? LeBlanc is thinking maybe Brayfield. Solid, young guy. In his second term, good constituency man, presents well, good speaker. Dartmouth born and bred. He'll go over well. It would be seen as a progressive move, whatever the hell that means."

"Christ, Brayfield? Has it come to that? The boy's not ready. I'm not sure he's strong enough to stand the heat when things gets cookin'. Not loyal enough either. I appreciate your chief of staff has put some thought into it, but there's gotta be better than young Dougie."

"Here's another thought, Dunc. I don't think you're going to like it much. Another of LeBlanc's ideas. Says our polling numbers are slipping badly with women. So how about Erin Curran?"

"I've got new shoes that have more political experience than her. Besides, there's MLAs like McCarthy and Oulton and Vandermark who've got two or three terms under their belts. Always done what was asked of them. Senior people who've never gotten a whiff of cabinet. They'll be pissed to be passed over again."

"We've got to put a new face on this party if we want to still be in power next time. I'd like to have one more term as premier, and I know you enjoy being a cabinet minister. LeBlanc and the boys figure this appointment is critical to making that happen. We need to get younger, more progressive, and more urban. Nothing says urban and new like a young woman."

"Maybe LeBlanc is right. You know me, I'm an old dog who believes in seniority. I'd rather have Erin than that straight-assed Brayfield. And she is a fine-lookin' young thing. A pretty face never hurt a political party. Fifteen years ago when they brought Janet Zwicker into the cabinet of the previous administration, I didn't think much of it, but you wouldn't believe how many older fellas back home took a shine to her. She was quite the looker in those days."

"Speaking of Janet, I've got to run this past her too. She'll be mad if I don't. And remember, it's about gender balance on the ticket. It's about giving urban women an important voice at the cabinet table."

"And it doesn't hurt that she's an urban voice with a fine ass on her."

"Dunc!"

"Don't worry, Premier. I'll stick to the talking points when the time comes. Hey, Premier, before you go, I gotta show you this app I got for my new iPhone. You're goin' to love it."

"I swear you know more about that damn phone of yours than half the millennials in my office."

CHAPTER 7

"Look, I'm not saying we're toast, I think we can turn it around, but the premier is going to have to jettison some of the dead wood."

"I totally agree, Doug. Just be more discreet about who you talk to about it. You can trust me and Nathalie, but be careful who else in caucus you say that to. Dunc has ears everywhere."

"You mean Jabba the Dunc?"

"Jabba the Dunc? That's funny, Doug," Nathalie says, flashing her wonderful grin that along with her brown eyes and dark brown hair, attracts as much attention as the positive energy that radiates from her. "But Erin's right, you've got to be careful. That guy knows everything. It's uncanny. His survival instincts are off the charts."

"One last round, guys? Hey, waiter, one more round, please. Thanks."

I love talking politics over drinks, and I'm enjoying the rare chance to do it with my two closest friends in caucus. Robbie is picking up Zoey from daycare, so I'm sitting back after my second Pinot Grigio, embracing the relaxing chatter at The Old Triangle as afternoon turns to evening.

We're an odd trio. Me, the daughter of a journalist and a teacher, coming off a handful of years in the non-profit sector after a few years in journalism. Doug, the son of a Dartmouth accountant, has a Dalhousie law degree and wanted something more than a comfortable legal career. And Nathalie grew up in a rural Acadian community and is a business executive whose father founded one of the most innovative international seafood companies in the province.

We're different in so many ways, yet similar in crucial ones. All three of us are fairly new to politics: Doug is in his second term, Nathalie is more than halfway through her first term, and I'm only a year in after winning a by-election. We're part of the progressive wing of the party and all forty or younger. Nathalie just turned the big four-O, Doug is thirty-five, and I'm thirty-six.

I'm an MLA because the party needed a sacrificial lamb to run in a district they hadn't won in a decade. Since none of our party's major players would risk taking on an Opposition rising star, the party reached out to me through Robbie. I'd been thinking about running for council in the next municipal election because I was frustrated by Halifax's planning decisions and the high density without appropriate green space that it was pushing on our area. So I saw the nomination as an opportunity to raise my profile for the next municipal election. The party hailed me as a sign of its commitment to run young female candidates, even though it was thought to be an unwinnable district. Only I surprised everybody and won.

Doug and Nathalie are wasted on the backbenches. Doug, a big, friendly guy who ran the Downtown Business Commission for years, has a great grasp on how this city works and is well respected. Before entering politics, Nathalie was the vice-president of her hard-driving father's company, in spite of being his daughter, not because of it. She's one of the savviest businesspeople around. She wanted to try something different before taking over the family business.

"Our government comes off as tired. We're halfway through our second term and we're out of ideas about what we want to accomplish. We've got no clear vision of why we want to govern, and that'll be obvious next election. We've got to reinvigorate ourselves. A dozen old white guys, a couple of unknown female ministers, and Janet Zwicker aren't going to make that happen. Janet might as well have honorary balls and a penis."

"You're right, Doug. If you're looking for a government to patch your rural road, we're your party. But if you want someone to fast-track Nova Scotia into the new economy or prepare for the demographic landslide of our aging population, you're going to vote for someone else."

"And we're not even talking about how screwed up things are municipally in this province. In some regions we have a different municipal government every few kilometres. You know, the premier should realize that promoting you two to cabinet would help us tackle all this stuff and solve the drift in our polling numbers. You guys are the Dynamic Duo, Super Evangeline and the Dartmouth Boy Wonder."

"You are a crazy woman. No wonder Robbie doesn't let you out on the town more often. I've got to go. Give him my love. Make sure you bring Zoey by the caucus office soon. That kid kills me. Bye, guys."

As Nathalie leaves, I hear a fiddle, a mandolin, and a guitar tuning up in the main room, around the corner from

"The Snug" where we're comfortably enjoying our drinks. Doug turns to me, his eyes serious.

"Erin, she'd be great in cabinet. No one there has even half her business experience. She's from southwestern Nova Scotia, Acadian, and female. The politics is a no-brainer. And don't sell yourself short. We only have one female cabinet minister from the city, and Grace, God love her, is as old as the Town Clock. We need a stronger female Halifax cabinet minister, and I think that some day that could be you."

CHAPTER 8

"What's her name again, Nada? The woman walking toward us."

"Julie, Julie Olatunji."

"Hi, Julie. Great to see you again. How are things? How are the boys settling in?"

"They like school. They learn English fast. I learn slowly."

I had met Julie and her two little boys a year ago at this same Immigrant Services Association Thanksgiving dinner shortly after they arrived from a war-torn part of Africa as refugees. Her husband had been killed in the fighting, and the family was hurting.

"And has Immigrant Services found you a job?"

"I work at hotel. Downtown. It is a good job. I like it."

Robbie signals me to come over to talk to someone who is with him. I give Julie a hug. She's come so far since we last met. This annual Thanksgiving event connects dozens of immigrant newcomers in our neighbourhood with local residents. It's one of my favourite community events. People from nearly thirty different countries in Africa, Asia, South

America, and particularly the Middle East mill about the elementary school gym. Julie's boys are running around with a gaggle of shrieking kids their age.

"I've got to go, Julie. Wonderful to see you. Can we take a quick photo of the two of us for my social media channels? Thanks."

Nada takes a picture with her phone and will post it shortly to my Twitter feed and Facebook page. I'm fairly active on social media. It's a great way to stay connected with people in my district, but it can come at a price that mostly only female MLAs pay. I've been called everything from a "bitch" to a "fucking feminist" by Twitter trolls. People don't hesitate to ask who is looking after my daughter, suggest that I look ugly wearing this or that outfit, or that I sound shrill. Some dude even said he'd like to see my head on a platter.

"Erin, this is Dr. Patel's mother, Noor. She's only been here for a few months and is trying to get used to the cold."

"Lovely to meet you, Mrs. Patel. Your son has been Robbie's GP for years. He speaks highly of him as a doctor and as a tennis partner. They play doubles together at Northcliffe."

"When he was younger, I had to drag Amit off the tennis courts all the time so he would go back to his studies," Mrs. Patel says, her face softening at the memories. "Now that he is a doctor, there's not much I can say. But I ask you, does he have to spend all his money on tickets to the US Open, the Canadian Open, and such? Better to invest his money. But he doesn't listen."

"Amit does love his tennis. Nice to meet you, Mrs. Patel."

Thank God this is a relaxed event and in my district. I'm able to dress more like myself in a blouse and slacks rather than my "uniform." Since I became an MLA, I've worn more blazers and skirts and boring pant suits than Hilary Clinton. As a female politician you can show style with colourful shoes or a vibrant scarf, yet that's as far as you can go. Absolutely nothing low-cut, provocative, or tight-fitting, which is why it's great to be out tonight in my multicoloured earrings with my usual bangles and bracelets.

Nada is heading toward me with Margot Beals from Immigrant Services, which is hosting this dinner as it has in the Fairview–Clayton Park area for nearly a decade. When I first started coming half a dozen years ago, there might've been fifty or sixty people here. Now more than two hundred pack the gym.

"Margot and I have been looking all over for you. Every time there's an Erin spotting, you turn in the opposite direction to chat with someone else."

"I know you spoke before dinner, but can you say a few words before the dance begins?" Margot asks.

Margot is the essence of grace under pressure. The past few years have been trying with the Syrian refugee crisis piled on top of ISA's regular work, but she marshals on. I borrow a mic from the band that's setting up to play some old-fashioned rock for the families settling in at tables spread around the gym.

"Folks, if I can have your attention. Again, I want to thank everyone for coming. I want to welcome the new Canadians and hope you're enjoying the chance to meet your neighbours. I want to thank those who've lived in this country for a long time, some their entire lives, for sharing our Thanksgiving traditions with our new friends. Also, a special thanks to the head of tonight's organizing committee, Ling Chow, and the rest of her committee. Thanks, Ling. We're very blessed in Fairview–Clayton Park to live in such a diverse community. New Canadians enrich and invigorate our culture and are a blessing to our province. It's an honour to represent you in the Nova Scotia Legislature, and believe me I love to sing the praises of the community we are building here, together. Enjoy the music."

As we make for the exit, Nada says, "Don't forget, Erin, you promised Lilly that you'd drop by the fundraiser for the Halifax West hockey team. Even if it's only for a few minutes."

"Robbie?"

"How about we pop in for half an hour so we can bid on something and you can show your face. Rick and Wendy will be there. Their son Ryan is on the team this year. I'll call your mom and tell her we're going to be home a bit later. Zoey is probably asleep by now, and your mom is likely watching a movie anyway."

"Okay, Nada. Thanks for everything. Don't be in a big rush to get in on Monday morning. You've been here for hours."

CHAPTER 9

As I turn off my laptop and head up to bed after a couple of hours of late-night reading, I'm struck by what an amazing life Joe had. He served as everything from premier to Lieutenant-Governor of Nova Scotia and was one of our first federal cabinet ministers after Confederation, rubbing elbows with Sir John A. Macdonald and George-Étienne Cartier. Nova Scotia sailing ships dominated British North American trade when he was young, and he lived to see the railroads and steamships that slowly eroded the wooden ships' trade. He saw Queen Victoria in London and visited Louis Riel's Red River Colony.

What amazed me most was that the famous libel trial against him was held in the Legislative Library where I first met him. When the trial took place in 1835, the room housed the Nova Scotia Supreme Court. So I suppose it's not surprising I saw him there, given the trial's importance in his life.

He faced a libel charge for a letter published on January 1, 1835, in his *Novascotian* newspaper signed by "The People."

It said Halifax magistrates and police had been picking the pockets of the poor for about one thousand pounds a year in excessive fines and schemes and that they'd been doing it for thirty years. The authorities charged Joe with "wickedly, maliciously, and seditiously contriving, devising, and intending to stir up and excite discontent and sedition amongst Her Majesty's subjects." Which sounds pretty bad, if a bit overdramatic.

In the 1830s it was libellous to publish anything calculated to degrade anyone or to "disturb the peace." Worse yet, the truth of the accusations or any absence of malice in making them weren't defences. Joe had stepped in it. The allegations were spot on, but that wasn't going to help him get off. Another nighttime sitting is coming, and I hope I'm able to connect with Joe to ask him about one of the most famous trials in Nova Scotia history.

"MY DEAR, it was an extraordinary event in the history of our beloved country and for me, as a young and untested man of public affairs. My publication of that letter started a conflagration of excitement in our fair city. The Government, the magistrates, and their friends could not wait to inflict punishment on so brazen a scoundrel as myself for daring to slander the King's justices and bringing into contempt the rulers of our land. I approached a handful of lawyers to take my case, and to a man they told me I had no case. They said there was no doubt the letter, written by my friend George Thompson under a *nom de plume*, was a criminal libel. They urged me to seek peace with the magistrates or face a fine and imprisonment."

"I read that even your good friend Thomas Haliburton thought the libel charge couldn't be beat."

"Quite so, even Tom, who would have gladly defended me were it not for the fact that he was a sitting judge. And so, despite my lack of legal training, I had no choice but to represent myself. One cannot embark on a journey with a helmsman at the wheel who does not believe in the course of your vessel. I borrowed books of law from my legal friends and holed up in my study, drinking endless cups of tea and reading libel law for more than a week. I schooled myself to do battle with more learned men who had attended King's College in Windsor and had proper legal training."

"Didn't you have doubts about the outcome of the trial? I know I'd have been worried sick."

"I must admit that on the eve of the trial, as my dear Susie and I walked through the new fallen snow over the Kissing Bridge and up the hill to Fort Massey, I had the most grave of doubts. As I looked down on the twinkling lights of Halifax, I feared not being able to properly present my argument, of losing the case and being separated from my wife and our adorable baby, Ellen. Fifteen years earlier a man who was convicted of a libel charge in Halifax was sentenced to two years hard labour at the Bridewell Prison, so I could envision what defeat might mean. Yet somehow, I was convinced that if I had the manly courage and powers of persuasion to put my case before a jury of twelve of my countrymen, they must acquit me. I thought that the majority of people wished in their hearts for my success but were convinced, as was I, that the Bench, the Bar, the Church, and every official and man of influence desired my conviction."

"So what was the trial like? It must've been incredibly intense."

"It was a whirlwind, a lightning bolt, a tempest. Absolutely exhilarating and positively exhausting, all in one. The courtroom was crammed to overflowing and hot as a furnace even though it was early March. Naturally, my one and only Susan Ann and my beloved father were there as well as friends and colleagues, but so too were many of the magistrates whom I had offended and their supporters, awaiting my comeuppance. No less a personage than Sir Brenton Halliburton, the Chief Justice of Nova Scotia, resplendent in his powdered wig and gown, was presiding judge. Of course, Halliburton was on the province's Executive Council, the one and the same council I regularly pilloried in my newspaper. In fact, he sat right over there where the librarian's desk rests now. Nova Scotia's Attorney General, S. G. W. Archibald, was my chief prosecutor. After being formally charged, I pled not guilty."

"So how did you lay out your case? It seems like they had you trapped in a corner with no way out. Where did you begin?"

"I began by demanding to know why I was charged with criminal libel in the first place. Why had not the magistrates charged me through a civil action? No doubt because it would give me a chance to prove my innocence by showing that the accusations against the magistrates were true, which I might do in a civil action but could not in a case of criminal libel. I said to the jury: 'Gentlemen, they dared not do it. I tell them in your presence and in the presence of the community whose confidence they have abused that they dared not do it. They knew that discretion was the better part of valour and that it might be safer to attempt to punish me than to justify themselves.'"

Joe is getting stirred up, his great white head animated, his bright blue eyes alert, his pale white skin colouring.

"I moved on to my argument in the main, that the magistrates were the most negligent, imbecilic, and reprehensible body that ever mismanaged a people's affairs and that before I was done with them, I hoped to convince the magistrates themselves that they, not I, were the real criminals."

Joe's language of the young rebel, willing to take on "the man," belies the image of the elder statesman before me.

"For the next six hours I defended myself and scourged my prosecutors, eliciting unbridled laughter from the onlookers, which the Chief Justice regularly brought to abrupt silence with authoritative raps of his ebony gavel. I built my case, brick by brick, until it was a veritable fortress. I cited all the magistrates' various schemes and collusions as they abused their positions and poorly managed the public money. Amongst their abuses, accounting books kept so poorly that no one knew where the money was and that those charged with running public institutions, like the prison and poorhouse, used their positions to enrich themselves."

Joe ticks off the offences on the thick fingers of his right hand as he names them.

"Some of the richest people in the city refused to pay taxes or debts and were never forced to pay them, while the poorest faced the full weight of the law for far lesser abuses. And fines paid to police and judges never made it to the public treasury but instead landed in the pockets of those very officials."

"Outrageous," I tell Joe, sharing his righteous anger. "The magistrates were absolute hypocrites. You were right to take them on."

"Indeed, I told the jury that I recognized that common

law forbade me from using the truth of the letter's accusations as my defence, yet argued that it was my duty to enunciate my state of mind in publishing it so that they could ascertain my real motive and intention and whether I was attempting to breach the peace or was actually labouring to restore and preserve it. At one point, I looked over at the jury box and saw one old fellow crying like a child, roused to high emotion by my words."

Joe grows silent, seemingly overcome at the remembrance of the scene.

"I argued that Nova Scotians deserved the very same rights as our fellow Englishmen across the great North Atlantic. Toward the end of my address, as late afternoon's shadows grew in the corners of the room, I stopped to gather myself. I mopped my damp forehead with my handkerchief and looked for Susan Ann's loving face in the public gallery before I summed up: 'Will you, my countrymen, the descendants of these men, warmed by their blood, inheriting their language, and having the principles for which they struggled confided to your care, allow them to be violated in your hands? Will you permit the sacred fire of liberty, brought by your fathers from the venerable temples of Britain, to be quenched and trodden out? Your verdict will be the most important ever delivered before this tribunal, and I conjure you to judge me by the principles of English law and to leave an unshackled press as a legacy to your children.' Grandiosely, I even insisted that if I were convicted of the charge, I would not desert my principles. 'Yes, gentlemen,' I said, 'come what will, while I live, Nova Scotia shall have the blessing of an open and unshackled press.' Perhaps, even I was carried away by my oratory."

It's like hearing Thomas Jefferson discuss his hopes for the US constitution, or a thirteenth-century English baron explaining the brutal politics behind King John's acceptance of the Magna Carta. Dad would be so jealous if he knew I was getting a blow-by-blow account of this famous Nova Scotia trial from the man at the centre of it. Robbie would be mesmerized.

"The Chief Justice adjourned the trial for the night after my lengthy address, and I was worried that the delay might lose whatever advantage I had gained. The next morning, after the Attorney General quickly summed up the case against me, Sir Brenton charged the jury with what sounded like the last nail in my coffin. Like an Old Testament judge he told them that the letter to the editor was a libel, I had published it, and their duty was to state by their verdict that it was libellous, before reluctantly adding that they were not bound by his opinion."

Joe, the consummate storyteller, pauses for effect. Even though I know the outcome, the suspense his retelling has built is intense. I can't wait to hear more.

"It took the jury ten minutes of deliberation to declare me not guilty with a unanimous verdict. The words stunned the courtroom into silence for a moment while everyone tried to grasp the immensity of the outcome. It was the falling away of the rusty chains of the old order, to be replaced by something shiny and new. Shouts rang out in the courtroom as pandemonium set in before spilling onto the streets. Everyone inside and outside hugged me, crushed my hand with vigorous handshakes, and gave me hearty slaps on the back. That evening in my bath my skin was black and blue from all the effusive congratulations. The crowd hoisted me onto their shoulders and carried me home. I was wonderfully, deliriously happy, but also spent."

A quietly satisfied smile spreads across Joe's face.

"For the rest of the day, Halifax celebrated my surprising

victory as most of the public, from all ranks and classes, were in my favour before the trial but with none imagining the outcome achieved. Even my most ardent newspaper competitors celebrated my victory in big black letters on their front pages."

For the first time since we began talking, I notice that a model of the scales of justice hangs on the wall behind Joe to memorialize the library's original use as a courtroom and as home to this famous trial.

"In the evening everyone turned out in their sleds for a torch-lit procession through the snowy streets and came to serenade Susie and me at our home. They called for us to come out, but frankly I was without the strength to join their revelry and with a short speech from my bedroom window I begged their leave to remain at home. The trial had taken every ounce of my manly vigour. I urged the crowd to keep the peace, to enjoy the triumph around their own firesides, and to teach their children the names of the twelve fine men of the jury who had established the freedom of the press."

"To take on the establishment like that was incredibly brave. Most people would never have taken on the challenge."

"Brave or foolish I had no choice, Erin, it was a matter of principle. Besides, as Master Shakespeare said: 'Cowards die many times before their deaths, the valiant never taste of death but once.'"

"So what was the result of your trial, besides clearing you of the libel charge?"

"The outcome was immediate, for it shook up the class of conniving crows who had helped govern our fair country since its founding while feathering their own nests. Several magistrates resigned, as did the commissioner for the poor.

The ruling families absolutely hated me now. Their women ran from me on the street, and the men plotted against me. One night one of their young fellows, well in his cups, rode onto the wooden sidewalk in front of the *Novascotian* with his sword drawn and started smashing the windows, shouting for me to come out. Well I did so. As I was in the midst of printing the newspaper, my hands and trousers were covered with ink. The swordsman took a drunken swipe at me before I grabbed the horse's bridle, grasped the attacker's wrist, and unarmed him. I pulled him from his steed and promptly knocked him out. You see, Erin, the pen is mightier than the sword."

Joe says this with such a devilish grin and dramatic flourish of his arms I can't help but laugh.

"A few months later, on one of my rambles through Nova Scotia looking for subscribers and to collect on overdue accounts, I realized that the outcome of the trial had given me a hold upon the hearts of the population that I had not imagined. And in Halifax itself, I could not go out to shoot a partridge in the woods or catch a trout in a stream without being suspected of canvassing for the next election, even though I did not run until two years later. I was even presented with a large silver pitcher at the Exchange Coffee House in Halifax by fellow Nova Scotians living in New York who sent it to me in honour of my defence of freedom of the press. The inscription said it was given as a testimony of their respect and admiration for my honest independence in publicly exposing fraud, improving the morals and correcting the errors of those in office, and for my eloquent and triumphant defence in support of the freedom the press. It was one of my most cherished possessions."

The torrent of words that flowed out of Joe for what

seemed like an hour halts. He takes a long pause, either from exhaustion or to emphasize a point.

"Most importantly, Erin, the trial gave me a glimpse of what I might become if I embraced a more ambitious vision of myself. Before the trial I was an indifferent public speaker known to stammer if especially nervous. Afterward, I was Howe, the skilled orator. Before the trial I was by parts courageous and by others outspoken. After the trial I embraced courage and outspokenness. My advice is that when opportunity knocks, answer the door. In order to embrace opportunity fully, you must become more of yourself. Look deep within and whatever you see as your finest qualities, your most constant strengths, exaggerate them within yourself, make them larger so that they are abundantly clear for all to see. Finally, I learned that the wise man does what events compel him to, whether he sees himself as up to the challenge or not. As the Roman philosopher Seneca said: 'Fate leads the willing, the unwilling it drags.'"

Without another word, Joe vanishes, leaving me to ponder the sudden turn of our conversation. Joe was only thirty-one years old when the trial took place, five years younger than I am. I can't imagine having such determination to achieve a goal.

I'm a high achiever who sets goals and often succeeds—winning a provincial debating championship, getting accepted into journalism school, attaining elected office—but I've never been so passionate about one objective that I gambled my whole future on it.

To brave the storm that Joe faced in the 1830s, taking on the powers that be, seems well beyond my abilities and my grasp—or is it?

CHAPTER 10

Since the end of the fall sitting of the Legislature, rumours have been flying around caucus and the media about a cabinet shuffle. Speculation has it that Dunc or Grace Smith will step down from cabinet, because they aren't expected to reoffer in the next election. Robbie thinks it would be great for the government if they both left. The benefit of Dunc's demotion is obvious and, in a way, so is a move with Grace.

She's a lovely woman and was the first person in caucus to reach out to me when I was elected, to offer advice about how to set up my constituency office. She's a hard-working MLA, but the combination of her age, late-sixties, and poor health are wearing her down. One-on-one in her district she's awesome. Outside in the broader world, she's a liability. Grace isn't tough enough to carry any of the heavy cabinet portfolios, which has left the city with few powerful cabinet ministers and none in the senior portfolios of Health, Community Services, or Finance. She's easily rattled in the House during Question Period and under media questioning.

Robbie and Doug are convinced that Nathalie has a good shot at being appointed, especially if Dunc gets dropped. It would be an even exchange of a rural mouse for a rural mouse. I think bringing in Doug to replace Grace would also be smart.

HAVE YOU HEARD ANYTHING? Am I in shit? I text Robbie minutes after I get a phone call to head to One Government Place and the Premier's Office for a quick meeting with him and LeBlanc, his chief of staff.

It's rarely a good thing to be summoned unexpectedly to the Premier's Office. I know I didn't handle government's rejection of a funding application for an organization in my district as well as I might have. I didn't connect with the group's president to calm her down before she went ballistic in the media. We ended up taking a public hit for a couple of days, and they probably blame me.

Heard nothing. Probably no biggie. In a meeting, Robbie texts, as I walk into the Premier's Office.

It's a spacious room with a big desk and large bay windows. An L-shaped sofa sits in one corner and small conference table in another. Nova Scotia landscapes hang on the walls and the coffee table has a handful of books by local photographers carefully fanned across it. It's nice but doesn't come close to the sophistication and opulence of the partners' offices in Robbie's law firm. LeBlanc looks up from one of her two cells as she sits alone on the sofa.

"Erin, thanks for popping by on short notice. Really appreciate it. Have a seat. The premier will be here in a minute. He's on his way back from speaking to the chamber of commerce. So how are things?"

LeBlanc has never said more than five words to me in my year in caucus. As usual she is stylin'. High heels that cost more than my entire outfit, matching handbag, and the latest cut from the most fashionable hair salon in the city. She's late forties, beautiful, yet severe. She never smiles and would gut you with one of her stilettos if it was in the premier's interests. I'm more anxious sitting here chit-chatting with her than I would be having a drink with the premier, who is about as easygoing as it comes, at least on the surface.

"Ah, Erin, good to see. Thanks for coming," the premier says as he walks in.

He's not a big man, probably five foot eight or so, late fifties with greying hair and a modest frame. He's not sophisticated or erudite, although he dresses well and is comfortable in his own skin. Ran a small-town car dealership with his father before entering politics and can make small talk with anyone.

"Sorry to bring you in here at the end of the day, I know you must want to get home for supper with Robbie, and what's your daughter's name? Uh, Zoey, right?"

"Yes, Premier."

"And how's our Robbie doin'? We sure miss him, but I know they have big plans for him over at MacKay and Macdonald, and from what I hear, he's doing well. Anyway, on to why we asked you to come over."

He pauses for a second, glances over at LeBlanc, who almost imperceptibly nods her head, and begins.

"As you know, Erin, we need to shuffle cabinet for a few reasons. Some personal issues for a few of our folks and also the need to freshen things up a bit in preparation for the next election. I don't know if you've heard that Bob is having some serious health issues again. He needs to step down from cabinet and focus on getting better. Naturally we all wish him the best. So that opened up one spot, and then Grace told us she's not going to reoffer next election, so that opens up another spot."

It's nice to be getting the inside scoop, still I wonder why the premier is telling a lowly backbencher like me.

"We've invited Nathalie Amirault to replace Bob in cabinet, and we're all excited about that. Her business experience will help us immensely. I'd also like to invite you to join cabinet, Erin, to replace Grace as minister at the Department of Health Promotion. You're young, up-and-coming, and will strengthen our cabinet team from Halifax. It's big shoes to fill. Grace is well liked in the party, but we feel you're the right person to do the job. So what do you say?"

I am speechless. I've never considered cabinet and I'm not sure I want the responsibility. I've only gotten a good grip on the basics of being a decent MLA and still have a lot to learn about government to be really useful to my constituents. From my limited time in elected politics, and from years of talking about it with Robbie, I know this kind of opportunity rarely comes. I also know that even though it's posed as a question, the premier expects to hear a yes— and I better say it quickly.

"Sorry, Premier, I don't quite know what to say," I stammer, not making a good impression as he and LeBlanc start to frown, "but I am honoured. I accept."

"Great, that's great. Welcome aboard," he says, as he stands and gives me a firm handshake. "I look forward to seeing you at cabinet."

LeBlanc walks around to my end of the sofa and gives me a stiff hug as though the act may permanently wrinkle her blouse. "We'll talk," she whispers in my ear. "Don't tell a soul yet, no one other than Robbie. A media release will go out first thing tomorrow."

I'm not sure how I get from One Government Place to my Volkswagen SUV parked outside Province House. There's a knot in my stomach as I pull my cell out, take a deep breath, and prepare to make one of the hardest phone calls I've ever made, to tell my husband that I've been appointed to his dream job.

CHAPTER 11

My head is spinning. After five days of briefings with my department's senior officials and reading hundreds of pages of reports, memos, fact sheets, and documents of every size, I'm exhausted. The amount of material I'm expected to have a handle on is massive.

I've had two or three multiple-hour briefings per day, with a handful of different department officials trooping into the minister's boardroom for each briefing. It's a revolving door of faces and issues. To help me grasp it all, staff put together my briefing bible, a binder on the department's structure, responsibilities, and programs that runs three hundred pages. Everyone stresses the need to keep it as tight as possible, yet after every briefing the deputy minister insists that it's crucial to add another handful of pages.

All this for Health Promotion, a small department that has a modest budget, about seventy employees, and is rarely in the news. I can't imagine the mountain of paper you'd have to climb to get up to speed at departments like Health, Education, or Community Services.

On top of my briefings, there's cabinet every Thursday morning plus caucus meetings and endless paperwork back at the office that requires my attention, ranging from grant approvals to key departmental decisions. I've written my signature so often that I feel like a Hollywood actor. I'm waiting for the paparazzi to jump out from behind a potted plant to take my photo.

Once I'm ready, I'll have meetings with stakeholders and speeches at conferences, announcements, and events. Somewhere in the midst of all that I'm expected to carve out two weekdays to be in my constituency office, plus attend the usual weekend and evening social events in the district.

It's a bit overwhelming, but the kindness others have shown me has helped. Doug sent Nathalie and me a hilarious email wishing us good luck and reminding us we're one banana-peel slip away from him taking our spot, complete with memes of cartoon pratfalls. Outgoing cabinet minister Grace Smith sent me a lovely, handwritten note on lavender stationery, and Robbie left a bouquet of orchids on my desk with a card that Zoey drew of me in front of an office building that stretched into the clouds.

On my third morning on the job, I decided to walk around the office and introduce myself to the staff, cubicle by grey cubicle. It's something I've done as a newbie wherever I've worked. It caused a stir. Some people told me they hadn't chatted one-on-one with the previous two or three ministers. Margaret Cameron, my deputy minister, looked upset when she arrived back at the office to find me talking with junior staff.

"Sorry, Minister, I didn't realize you wanted to do a walkabout. I would've arranged to introduce you around to our people and explained what each of them is responsible for. You could have been more prepared."

I don't know what to make of Margaret. She's early sixties, a career public servant, and one of the first female deputies from back in the day when there were hardly any compared to now when female deputies outnumber men two to one.

"No problem, Margaret. Nothing I can't do on my own. I didn't want to bother you, and really I never thought to do it until I walked in the door."

Ever since, I've had the sense that she is watching me, trying to decide whether I'm going to be one of those erratic or eccentric ministers that she has to keep a close eye on.

So far, I've been impressed with the staff. They're bright, well-educated—most with at least an undergraduate degree and many with a master's—and passionate about what they do. Everyone's deference to me feels weird though, especially calling me "Minister," despite my insistence several times that I'm "Erin." My every desire—more coffee, some water, how I like information presented to me, what works for my schedule—is accommodated. I was the executive director of a small charity before running for office and had more of a first-among-equals leadership style with my three staff. Here I have been crowned Queen.

"Great work, folks," Margaret says after most briefings. "Good presentation. We'll need to fine-tune a couple of those briefing notes. I've got a few context pieces I'd like you to add that we can talk about offline. No need to bother the minister with the details until we get them polished up."

She's a big, red-headed woman with a sharp mind. She's soft-spoken yet commands the respect of her staff, who seem to value her, like you appreciated that strict junior high teacher who always had your best interests at heart.

This is the fourth department she's headed, and rumour is she's about a year out from retirement. I think she's one of the reasons I got assigned to Health Promotion. The Premier's Office must've thought that someone needed to hold my hand while I learned the job, and she's the perfect choice.

Also, this department is out of the public's eye. None of the party's big platform commitments touch on us, and the PO wants to keep it that way.

I'm halfway through my second careful read of the briefing bible when I hear a knock and look up to see the deputy standing in the doorway.

"Sorry to disturb you, Minister. I thought I'd pop in and see how your first week has gone."

"Your folks have buried me in paper, so I'm trying to dig out."

"You've done a lot of reading. Staff have been impressed. They're not used to the minister actually reading their briefing materials, let alone doubling back to ask more questions after they've been briefed. Our last couple of ministers were not as engaged."

She smiles as she says "engaged."

"I guess that's my way. I assume all this content was developed for a good reason. It obviously took a lot of time and effort to distill all this complicated material into something a newbie like me can understand."

"Don't worry if you don't have it all mastered right away. It will take months to feel comfortable. You're doing well, Minister. With the House not in session, we shouldn't face any real tests until well into the new year. You have some time."

She smiles again and leaves me to my briefing bible. I glance at the photos on my desk of me and Robbie smiling on a beach in the Dominican, of Zoey on a mall Santa's lap, and of me with Mom and Dad on the steps of King's College at convocation. Sitting in this big empty office as Friday afternoon turns to evening, time is the one thing I feel I have little of these days.

CHAPTER 12

Energy dances in the air. It hops and skips a breath above the runners milling about in front of the Public Gardens. I look for familiar faces among the hundreds, and seeing none I find a patch of grass and begin my pre-race stretches.

Muffled instructions from a sound system interrupt the easy banter of the runners and stop songbirds in the trees mid-chorus. Elite runners with long limbs, slim torsos, and the graceful strides of gazelles congregate at the starting line, back from three-kilometre warm-up runs at paces that are exhausting to watch.

They glow with the confidence of athletes, sure in the knowledge of what their bodies can do. Most are in their twenties or early thirties and childless. The single gazelles circle around each other in a mating ritual out of BBC's *Planet Earth*. You can almost hear Sir David Attenborough quietly describing the scene. "It's as though they are saying to each other: 'I'm healthy, you're healthy, so why don't we get together and spread our DNA?'"

I don't have the long, tapered legs of a runner. I'm

thicker through the thighs, even though at five foot eight I'm as tall as some of the better long-distance runners that are here. This is the last time I'll see the elite runners until the finish line. By the time I'm done they will be chatting with friends as if they just came back from a stroll to Starbucks for a grande dark roast. I'll look like an escapee from a Southern prison farm after a night in the swamps—beet red and sweaty.

I'm totally unprepared for this ten-kilometre race, the last one of the fall. My life with Robbie and Zoey before I entered cabinet gave me a little time to squeeze in the occasional run, but now it's virtually impossible. It's another item on the growing list of things I don't have time to do right. "Better half-assed than never" is my new motto. I used to be such a perfectionist.

I find my place in the last third of the runners. People of every body size and age, all of us struggling to stay fit, fight bulges and aches. An air horn sounds and we're off in a fizz of euphoria as hundreds of people uncork the energy bottled up inside. Running in a large crowd unnerves me, with strangers invading my personal space. My running is solitary and meant to be.

Past the one-kilometre mark and I doubt I will make it to two. I am tight and fighting for breath. I feel a pull in my left calf I've never felt before. It should be going better than this. I squeeze past a guy with spidery hair on his back spilling out of a too tight muscle shirt. Here I go, falling into a more relaxed rhythm. There, open pavement. Feel better, lungs working, legs find their stride.

Hello, look at that ass. A beautiful ass and two sculpted legs. Michelangelo would be proud. I think I'm going to follow that ass for the next seven kilometres. I could run on and on behind him. Forget for a minute about the family and the grind of responsibility. My mind relaxes, stretches itself loose, remembering a time before my tummy grew stretch marks and my boobs headed south.

Loading up on beer and cheap wine in our residence rooms at Dalhousie and then heading downtown to the bars with my friends on a Saturday night. All of us looking great, feeling great. Dancing the night away without a care, the music flowing through our bodies, the beat mindless and consuming. Maybe getting picked up by some guy in the midst of it all and ending up at his place. Going with the moment. Sometimes it's good, sometimes it isn't. Laughing at the night's excesses the next morning over breakfast at Mary's Place Café II with my friends.

We run down South Park Street all the way to Point Pleasant Park, turn left and work our way onto the paths. The five-kilometre mark is beside the anchor planted along the shore. I feel great. My arms are loose, pumping above my hips. My legs are relaxed and my calf muscle is fine. The harbour between the park and McNabs Island is smooth as jello and gently jiggling. I have the heels of Achilles. I am a Mi'kmaw warrior sprinting along a deer trail. I could run on and on.

I've been reading more about Joe, and something he wrote in the *Novascotian* as a young man pops into my head. Headlined "Petticoat Government," it may have been tongue-in-cheek, although Joe did seem well ahead of his time in his relationship with his wife, Susan Ann. Joe said he'd be happy to let women govern the world for the next one hundred years, as he thought men had tried their hand at it long enough and had made a mess of things. He said women couldn't do much worse and that he expected they would do a whole lot better.

He suggested that wars would be eliminated, duelling

would disappear in a week, and drunkenness would be put down by depriving delinquents of all social and political privileges for twelve months for each offence.

In another column Joe asked rhetorically whether nature didn't intend women to do more than curl their hair, look after children, and make pies. He wondered whether there wasn't any literary or scientific pursuit that might enhance their intellect without interfering with their domestic activities.

I look up and that ass is taking off at warp speed. I must be starting to fall apart again. My new running bra chafes. I should've worn the old one.

Cable Hill looms with a steep incline that saps strength and crushes my ego. Like an afternoon spent shopping with Mom. I dig in on the balls of my feet, using my quads and hamstrings to pull me up the sandy path. I pant, draw air into my lungs, and push it out. As I crest the hill, I pay the price for this explosive use of energy. My stomach muscles constrict in reaction to an invisible punch. My head feels woozy. The feeling recedes as the hill falls behind me.

Robbie and Zoey will be at the finish line, vampires waiting to devour what little time and energy I have left. For a few more precious moments I'm free. Free to think about me and my life. To try and remember what my needs were before "my" was replaced with "our." Our plans, our roles, our needs.

The seven-kilometre mark, time to bear down. My legs are okay, but I can feel the lactate creeping into my muscles, stiffening the gears. There's no more chatting among the runners, only the echo of hundreds of footfalls on pavement. Past the Subway at the corner of Robie Street and Spring Garden Road that was once a deli and the only place you could buy a copy of the Sunday *New York Times*.

I would wake up, put on Robbie's Blue Jays ballcap over my uncombed sex hair, and walk over to buy a paper from the scowling Greek owner. Robbie would make coffee and we'd crawl back into bed to read, talk, and screw the afternoon away. I can't remember the last time we did that.

My tank is nearly empty as we run past the leafy Camp Hill Cemetery. From the shadows its ancient residents laugh at our folly, including Joe who rests under an engraved column of Nova Scotia granite. He passed away in 1873, but nearly died more than forty years earlier, not long after he bought the *Novascotian*.

Joe came down with a high fever after a hectic, afternoon-long game of doubles at the Garrison Racquet Court. His friend, Dr. Grigor, thought the situation was so bad that he gathered Joe's family and friends around his bedside to say goodbye. Of course, Joe had the constitution of a workhorse and rallied back to good health. God knows what Nova Scotia would've been like if he hadn't survived to fight his famous libel trial and to help bring us responsible government.

I jog past the Wanderers Ground and the Public Gardens' greenhouses toward the corner of Sackville and South Park. As I pass the spiked, wrought iron fence that guards the Public Gardens, I worry that I might wobble over and smash into it. I can see the finish line but can't pick up my pace. At best, I hope to finish the race still running.

Done, at last. The left side of my brain wonders why the right side feels fuzzy. I have the legs of a drunken sailor. Someone points me toward the finish line chute and hands me a paper cup with water that I gulp down with a gag. I can see them. Zoey dashes away from Robbie and bolts herself to my leg, her little body hot as a furnace.

"Mommy, you did it. You beat lots of other mommies."

"Well done, must be your best time ever," Robbie says, as he hugs me, the growing beer gut that warms my back at night pressing into my damp running shirt. I'm sweaty, tired, and lugging around a clammy three-year-old who wants a drink from one of the little paper cups like Mommy. Robbie's gone to get the car that, as usual, he parked blocks away. I haven't had time to cool down or stretch. I'll pay for that tomorrow.

We walk past a gazelle girl lounging on the grass. She is in her late twenties, without a bead of perspiration on a body that's barely hidden in the latest two-piece running outfit. Flat tummy, tight bum, firm breasts. An amazon, awaiting her reward. Maybe the bronzed Adonis with the ass. She looks our way, sees Zoey, and beams, captured by my daughter's elfin glow. She slings her gym bag over her shoulder, glances about for anyone she knows, puts her head down, and walks away, alone.

For a moment, walking with Zoey down the sidewalk through the fallen leaves, I feel great. I grab her hand and we go into the runner's tent for the after-race wedges of watermelon that Zoey will smear all over her cherub face. I smile at the thought.

CHAPTER 13

It's been weeks since I was last in the Legislature. The session is over and I'm spending ridiculous hours at my new department, trying not to let my constituency work slip while also attempting to get some face time with Robbie and Zoey.

I've ducked in here under the pretense of needing half an hour to catch up on emails as the first flakes of winter turn downtown Halifax into a snow globe. The security guards looked at me oddly. They know I have an office only blocks away. I tell them it was too slippery to walk up the hill. It's working hours and so the library has a couple of librarians and a party researcher milling about. I head downstairs to the Veterans Room.

It's my favourite place on the ground floor, with cream-coloured walls and curtains, Sheraton chairs, and a large dining table. It's like something out of *Downton Abbey*. Twenty years ago this space was still the Cabinet Room. I'm hoping I can connect with Joe, as the first time I saw him it was here. I have so much to talk about. I've been here for about ten minutes when suddenly my feet turn ice cold. The room fills with the pungent aroma of a cigar.

I look around, expecting to see some security guard who snuck in for a smoke break. There is no one. In the corner, near the door to the adjoining Johnston Room, a wisp of smoke appears. Out of it walks a man in nineteenth-century clothes. It isn't Joe. He is younger and bulkier with a full beard and a top hat. He wears a dark frock coat and a light vest.

I'm surprised and afraid, although the apparition's manner isn't threatening.

"You're not Joe. Who the hell are you?"

"No, madam, I am not the Honourable Joe Howe. I am his aide, friend, and companion in this afterlife. Ennis Douglas at your s-s-s-service."

He doffs his hat and makes a slight bow. I nod in return, not quite sure what the proper way is to greet a ghost, given he's only the second one I've met.

"Where's Joe? I wanted to chat. I've missed seeing him. I've so much to discuss with him."

"He is indisposed at the moment. Not his usual self. He has missed your company, and I believe it weighs heavily on him."

"Oh God, he's not ill, is he?"

"Not ill, madam, we do not get ill. I would describe his affliction as being more out of sorts. He has cherished your recent conversations, and so when they stopped without warning, it was quite the shock to his s-s-system. You must appreciate that for Joe it was a delight to have a new person to talk with after a century and a half of conversing only with me."

"You mean in all that time he's not been able to connect with anyone else who is living?"

"He has not."

"But why after all these years? Why has he been able to connect with me, Mr. Douglas?"

"Who can say, madam. All I know for certain is that t-t-talking with you has greatly revived his spirits, which have been in the doldrums for decades."

"Go tell him I'm here and apologize for my rudeness at not coming sooner. I've been appointed to cabinet and have been crazy busy."

"I am sorry, but it does not work in that way. I will let him know that you called on him, and that alone will greatly revive his spirits. He has found your political discussions quite invigorating. You know, it is a shame that you could not have met Joe in his prime. He was a true force of nature. He had the...he had the s-s-stamina of an ox and the courage of a lion. He was the wittiest fellow one could ever meet and insatiably curious. A friend to men of all races, colours, and creeds, with contempt for humbugs. When he saw silly male peacocks strutting about, he liked to ruffle their feathers. Sadly, you have met only a shadow of that great man."

"Naturally, I've read about him, but it's hard to get a true feel of a person from books."

Ennis pauses, stroking his beard thoughtfully.

"You should have seen him in his element, at a summer-time political picnic, whether it was in Hants County, Annapolis Royal, or the Musquodoboit Valley. It would tell you everything about the man."

"Please, go on."

"Families supportive of our party eagerly awaited such opportunities to meet Joe and our other political leaders and to break bread with their neighbours in an age when there were few entertainments in rural Nova Scotia. Liberal leaders like Howe, A. G. Archibald, William Young, and William Annand would arrive in a carriage festooned with Liberal colours and be formally met by the leading men of the district. Joe, of course would have already fled the official party and was walking among the crowd sitting on their p-p-picnic blankets, calling out to one and all by their Christian names. Wherever he went he knew most people because of his rambles. He would good-naturedly hug and kiss nearly every woman he met and their older daughters, too. One would see him squiring about with one country wife on his arm and then another, stopping by various families to share some of their victuals from their overflowing p-p-picnic baskets."

"And what year was this, Ennis? Give me a sense of when you're talking about."

"This could have been any summer between 1837 and 1867 but particularly in the forties and fifties when Joe's star sh-sh-shone so brilliantly.

"Now where was I? Eventually the Liberal luminaries gathered on a makeshift stage in the middle of the field to speak, but of course Joe would be missing. He was inevitably found, dashing about with a chicken drumstick in his hand, and pushed toward the stage. Archibald, Young, and Annand spoke first, pontificating on the important issues of the day in formal and sometimes long-winded speeches, but the crowd always wanted Joe."

Ennis feels around in the pocket of his vest and pulls out a cigar. He pats the same pocket, in search of matches, before looking up sheepishly, like a little boy caught stealing a crab apple from the neighbour's tree, a blush colouring his dour features.

"My apologies, madam. It is inappropriate to smoke in front of a young lady. I have been too long in only Joe's company. As I was saying, normally Joe would begin with some joke or witticism. A joke I heard many times went something like this: 'The history of wine is curious. Its invention is attributed to Noah, who certainly had seen enough of the evils of water.' Or, on a similar theme, he would speak on issues of the day such as one once popular in Maine, a bill to promote the prohibition of alcohol. 'The world has come down to the present period from the most remote antiquity with the wine cup in its hand,' Joe would say. 'David, the man after God's own heart, drank wine. S-S-Solomon, the wisest of monarchs and human beings, drank wine. Our saviour not only drank it, but commanded Christians to drink it in remembrance of Him. All the orators of antiquity and of modern times indulged in the juice of the grape.'"

Ennis takes off his top hat, revealing a head of thinning brown hair, and carefully lays it on the table.

"Joe went on: 'Let one's eye range through the noble galleries where the sculptors have left their statues, where the painters have hung in rich profusion the noblest works of art. Wine, we are told, clouds the faculties and deadens the imagination. Yet it was drunk by those benefactors of their race, and we cannot, with the masterpieces before us, believe the assertion, until their works have been eclipsed by artists trained up under this prohibitive legislation. Has Maine turned out as yet a statue that anybody would look at? A picture that anybody would buy? Look at the heroic defenders of nations. Was Washington a member of the temperance society? Did not Wallace drink the red wine through the helmet barred?'"

The story of Joe on the picnic circuit is amusing, but it's like hearing it told by the straight man in a comedy duo rather than the funny one.

"'If then, ladies and gentlemen, all that is valuable in the past—if heroism and architecture and oratory, sculpture and painting—if all that has bulwarked freedom and embellished life has come down to us with the juice of the grape, if no age has been long without it, I think it behooves the advocates of this prohibition to show us some country where their system has been tried; some race of men who drank nothing but cold water.'"

His sad eyes contain a trace of a smile, the faintest hit of a grin begins at the corners of his plump lips.

"Or Joe would take the opportunity to needle our p-p-political opponents with a barb suggesting his opponents in the Legislature were eloquent enough and would be almost as much so if their heads fell off, provided that their lungs remained. Or, he'd quote his favourite, Shakespeare, and say his political foes had no more brains than he had in his elbow. Always the most ardent Nova Scotian, Joe played on the crowd's patriotism. 'Boys,' he would say, 'brag of your country. When I am abroad, I brag of everything that Nova Scotia is or has or can produce, and when they beat me at everything else I turn around and say—how high do your tides rise?' That was Joe through and through."

Ennis leans against one of two plush, red chairs that frame a fireplace whose mantel commemorates Admiral Nelson's victory at Trafalgar.

"After warming the crowd with humour, he would move on to grab their hearts with eulogies to recently departed members of their community, all of whom he knew. Only once he had t-t-t-tickled the crowd's sides with humour and engaged their hearts did he move on to the meat of his oration. He had a way, madam, of throwing back his frock coat before he launched into the main portion of his speech that excited the crowd, especially in rural Nova Scotia, where they could look forward to dazzling wordplay rarely heard in their plain and quiet world. Joe never disappointed, speaking with a combination of eloquence and ribaldry that always transferred his enthusiasm for an idea to his audience. Afterward, they would swear to a man that it was one of the finest ideas they had ever heard. Throughout it all, Joe had the crowd, young and old, in the palm of his hands, bringing them from shaking fits of laughter and t-t-tears to thunderous enthusiasm like the conductor of a London orchestra."

Ennis halts, a wistful look on his face, as though recounting those scenes had transported him back to far better times.

"Thank you for telling me all this. It's so different to hear about Joe from a friend and colleague. You've given me a much better sense of him. It's been lovely to meet you, but I've got to run. I didn't realize the time. I'm going to be late to pick up my daughter again. My apologies. Say hi to Joe for me."

CHAPTER 14

A few months ago, this scene would've seemed ridiculous. Like something out of a 1950s screwball comedy that my dad loves to watch on TCM. I'm sitting in the Legislature's Nova Scotia Reception Room, a space used for welcoming small groups of dignities and guests. I'm waiting for the historical Joe Howe to arrive out of thin air, which I know he will. It's become so normal that I forget how insane it is.

The tang of copper coats my tongue as Joe takes shape. He's standing by an antique grandfather clock, which rests between two large windows. I've only talked to Joe a few times, yet each time he seems a little livelier. He turns his gigantic old head and looks at the clock face.

"You know this beautiful piece was made by Alexander Troup, of the Halifax Troups. Beautiful craftsmanship, typical of our fine Nova Scotian craftsmen. No one like them in the world. If I recall, old Troup had a comely daughter too."

"I'm sorry I haven't been able to see you lately, Joe. Being a cabinet minister has swallowed my private life and all my days. I hardly have any time to spend with my family."

"Life in senior political positions has that effect, most regrettably. I did not know you had a family. I confess I presumed a woman with a young family would be unable to take time to hold a cabinet post."

"Our times are very different. I'm married, my husband, Robbie, is a lawyer, and we have a daughter, Zoey, who's three years old. We share the parenting duties."

"My word, you have a little girl. Delightful. How I envy you. Oh, to hear a little one's laugh again, without a care in the world, to bounce them on your knee. I miss it so. You are blessed."

"You're right. I wish I could figure out how to spend more time with her and Robbie. I get up before she wakes, not easy with a toddler, and work after she's gone to bed. I only get a few precious hours a day with her at best. My half-hour reading to Zoey, cuddled close, her head on my shoulder, is the best part of my day. That and listening to her soft breath as she falls asleep. Of course, that doesn't mean she sleeps through the night."

"Why, I remember putting baby Ellen to sleep. Coming back from my various jaunts, weeks on the road, thinking of nothing but her smile, her bubbly coos, and her mother, my darling Susie. After nearly two hundred years, I recall it as if it were yesterday."

"I'll show you some pictures of Zoey and Robbie, I've got dozens on my phone. Ah, here's one taken a few weeks ago. They're playing with a toy tea set Mom gave her, and she's pouring some for her favourite doll, which she named Dolly. And there's this one of her dressed as Peppa Pig to go out trick-or-treating at Halloween. Doesn't she look cute?"

I hold my phone up to Joe so he can see the screen.

"I am afraid that I am unable to see anything on those devices you all carry in your hands and find so devilishly fascinating. I have the same problem with those boxes with the small window and buttons in the front that are placed here and there in Province House. Ennis finds he cannot see or hear anything emanating from them either. Years ago there were smaller boxes with dials but without screens that obviously emitted some form of sound, yet we heard nothing."

"So you can't see or hear what's on TV or a phone or hear a radio? Wow."

The thought of not being able to use any electronic media is both horrifying and vaguely intriguing. To be that unconnected feels almost naughty.

"So what about you and Susan Ann? Did you have a large family?"

"We had twelve children, but only six lived to be adults. Our first baby did not. That was painfully sad, the loss of all of our children was terrible, but Susan Ann was made of strong stuff. She was the daughter of Captain John McNab of the Nova Scotia Fencibles, an infantry regiment, so she and her mother had learned the toughness of those who have followed the drum."

"And how did you two meet?"

"One Sunday I saw Susie and her family walking to St. Paul's to attend service. Her charming little nose and hazel eyes captured me the moment I laid eyes on her. And she smiled at me as she passed. Even though I was raised by my father as a Sandemanian, dissenters from the Church of England, I found myself trailing behind them to St. Paul's. After that, I spent a great many evenings rowing back and forth to McNabs Island. Good or choppy seas, it mattered not. Some of the most precious evenings of my life were those whiled away with Susie, worshipping the moon under a canopy of trees on that island paradise.

"'Thou canst remember—canst thou e'er forget
While life remains, that placid summer night
When, from the thousand stars in azure set,
Stream'd forth a flood of soft subduing light
And o'er our heads, in Heaven's topmost height,
The moon moved proudly, like a very Queen,
Claiming all earthly worship as her right,
And hallowing, by her power, the peaceful scene
Spread out beneath her smile, so tranquil and serene.'"

"That's lovely. Who wrote it?"

"A Nova Scotia poet, actually, by the name of Joseph Howe."

"I'm sure your wife loved it. Wait a second, your wife lived on McNabs Island? She was a McNab from McNabs Island? I don't think anyone has lived on the island since the Second World War. I see it some days on my way to work, shyly poking out from behind Georges Island, but I've never been there. Robbie and I mean to go every summer and never seem to manage it."

"I was blessed to marry dearest Susie at St. Paul's in the winter of 1828, not long after taking over the *Novascotian*, at which point her family thought I had sufficient future prospects to be acceptable. This despite entering the marriage with an illegitimate son, Edward, my first-born whom my family and I chose to raise after my unfortunate dalliance with a young woman. Dearest Susie treated Edward like her own child from the moment she saw him and welcomed him into our home, God bless her. Besides Edward, we had six children who gained adulthood, the girls—Mary and Ellen—and four boys: Joseph, Frederick, William, and Sydenham."

"That's a houseful of kids. They must have kept you and Susan Ann busy."

"Delightfully busy. Our Fred served in the Army of the North during the American Civil War, first as a private in a New York infantry regiment and later as a corporal with the 23rd Ohio Regiment. Miraculously he escaped unscathed from some of the bloodiest battles of that horrible war. In the spring of 1865 when I travelled to Washington and met the new president, Andrew Jackson, Fred and I toured the courtroom where John Wilkes Booth's conspirators in President Lincoln's assassination were being tried. It was an emotional time to be visiting the capital of the United States of America. Wonderful to see my boy, yet I confess Fred looked a decade older after all the horrors he had witnessed. Dear Sydenham, the last of my children to walk the mortal earth, did a great deal to preserve my papers and documents for posterity. Warts and all, they are there for all to see."

Joe slowly fades away, a sad smile on his face.

As I'm packing up to go, I feel a chilling draft accompanied by a pungent whiff of cigar tobacco.

"Susan Ann was a most extraordinary and unique woman."

I turn in my chair to see Ennis Douglas standing beside an antique secretary bookcase filled with Mi'kmaw artifacts. He looks so sombre you'd think he'd just come from a family funeral. I have no way of knowing whether he's always been like this, but I suspect he has.

"Theirs was a wonderful p-p-partnership and far more equal than anyone imagines. They did not think exactly alike and yet had a similar point of view. It was not uncommon for them to initially disagree. Susan Ann was always discreet about airing these differences publicly, yet amongst family and those who worked with Joe, she never hesitated. They would have these little disagreements before reaching a consensus and then move on as though nothing had happened. They had the greatest mutual respect that I have ever had the privilege to witness."

"Ennis, knowing what you know about the times I live in, what do you think Susan Ann would've done or achieved in our era?"

"Anything that she set out to do. In your time I can see her sitting in this very Legislature, if she chose to, operating a large mercantile firm, or running a p-p-provincial newspaper. Often when Joe was away, she and I ran the *Novascotian*, she as much as I. What is more, she did this while looking after the children and balancing the family's always precarious finances like a ringmaster in a three-ring circus. She was also a careful and dispassionate observer of people, including Joe himself. She knew his strengths and weaknesses, and what's more, Joe accepted her wisdom in these matters. He also found her assessments of others invaluable, even if at times he did not use that information as well as he might have done."

"She sounds amazing. I would've loved to have met her. History teaches us a lot about the great men of your era but very little about the extraordinary women."

"On a personal note, she always offered a kind and sympathetic ear to someone like myself who relied on her discretion, advice, and support."

Ennis departs and I'm left with a warm glow, my faith in the power of love reaffirmed. After all Joe's years of reflection on a full life, his love of Susan Ann and the family they built together burns brightest. A cooing baby Ellen. A starry night long ago with his dearest. It is the truest poetry of his life.

The other day, a car in front of me on the Bedford Highway had a bumper sticker that read: Life doesn't last forever, but love does. I only hope that Robbie and I are building the kind of life together for our family that Joe and Susan Ann created.

CHAPTER 15

Robbie isn't handling my being in cabinet well. As a former executive assistant to two ministers, one ambitious and responsible, the other coasting to retirement, he knows the maximum and minimum amount of time required to do the job. It's one thing to be the eager twentysomething executive assistant with no responsibilities supporting the minister and quite another to be a husband putting the minister's daughter to bed or having to rush out of important business meetings to grab Zoey at daycare when my day goes sideways. The partners at his law firm are starting to notice, and not in a good way.

Summer thinks Robbie is being a typical man, sulking because he's not in the limelight while his woman is the centre of attention. She cites it as reason number seventeen that she's a lesbian.

"For fuck's sake, Curran, it's about time he carried more of the load for Zoey and for all the housework bullshit. If you and Robbie the Robot are going to lead the boring, uber-successful, suburban life that he's always wanted, it comes at a price. This time it's his turn to pay."

All this is frustrating for a career-orientated guy like Robbie, but what's killing him is that I'm doing the job he's dreamed of his whole adult life. He's the political animal, not me. I like what politics can achieve under the right circumstances; I put up with the crap by keeping the outcome in mind.

My husband loves everything about politics. The adrenalin rush of battles between our party and other parties. Laying traps for political opponents. Being in on the latest gossip. All the old war stories of politics back in the day. Comparing and contrasting various policy options. Creating something out of nothing and helping to improve people's lives.

His passion for it made him stand out from the rest of the twentysomething guys I ran into at downtown Halifax bars and parties when I was a young journalist. There were some crazy-handsome athletes, plenty of good-time guys, and some funny dudes who were hilarious to hang with, but Robbie's intensity attracted me. He already knew what he wanted, and that made him way more centred than the competition.

When we met, he was working in the party's caucus office as a researcher. He hadn't become an EA yet. We kept running into each other through mutual friends. I enjoyed being around him but was coming off a long-term relationship and thought I needed a break. So much for that. He was so engaged with everything going on in the province and the world that pretty soon I fell for the guy.

The other thing that attracted me was his passion for music. From Counting Crows to Rage Against the Machine and Public Enemy, to B.B. King and Diana Krall. Even Bach and Chopin. Robbie got this otherworldly look on his face when he listened that was so gentle and open and sexy.

My husband always says the first thing he noticed about me was my smile. He liked my hazel eyes too, which are green in some light, brown in others. And he liked how clearly I expressed myself, something people have always told me. Only after we'd been together for a while did he mention another of my features that attracted him.

"Erin, you have a great ass. All the guys we hung out with when we first met thought you had one of the nicest asses in Halifax, and you know what? They're right."

After a few weeks we were seeing each other regularly and exclusively. It was insane. One weekend early in our relationship we went to bed on a Friday night and didn't get out until Sunday evening. We couldn't get enough of each other. We'd make out, talk, eat in bed, read, watch TV, make out, talk, fall asleep, wake up, check our phones, and make out again. It was madness. I was sore for days afterward.

We'd been seeing each other for a couple of months when one night after a wild party we weaved home to my place. Robbie was drunker than I'd ever seen him. He was always fun, yet after spending time with him I came to realize that he drank way less than the rest of us, and certainly less than me. He always had a beer in his hand, but it was usually the same one. After having boyfriends who'd get stumbling drunk, it was a nice change.

"Erin, I got to tell you somethin'," he said, as we sat on the bed in my tiny, downtown Halifax, bachelor apartment. "It's somethin' you need to know about me. I want you to know because I want everything to be straight up with us."

He looked so serious I didn't know what to think. Did this wonderful guy have a secret love child back home in Ontario? Had he been kicked out of university for cheating on exams? I had this awful feeling that this wonderful ride was about to end.

"The summer after I graduated from high school, I spent lots of time at my parents' place in cottage country. It's a great place and I had a lot of fun, too much fun. One night me and my buddies were partying and ran out of beer. They talked me into taking our boat across the lake to get some more at Chad's cottage. It was a warm summer evening, near midnight. There was no moon and it was pitch black on the lake. We were blasting along with the music blaring when out of nowhere a boat appears in our forward lights. Dad's boat was big, a 45-foot cabin cruiser, and heavy. The other boat was a 14-foot aluminum fishing boat. We crushed through it like a pop can. Next thing I knew, Chad was yelling and holding an arm with a piece of bone sticking out, and there was screaming from out in the blackness. At first, I wasn't even sure the screams were human. The crash knocked out our boat lights. Eventually we found a flashlight and spotted two girls thrashing around in the water and fished them out. But there had been three girls in that boat, Erin. Three. The police didn't find the other girl's body until the next day. She was dead. Died on impact, the coroner said. She was eighteen, the same age I was, and she was dead."

I remember turning to the window and looking into the treed darkness of a wintry Victoria Park. It was as bleak as I had ever seen it.

"At first I was charged with manslaughter until Dad got control of the situation. I told you Dad was a lawyer, but he's not any lawyer. He's the Morrison of Morrison, Bernstein, Nakamura."

"The big Toronto law firm? Wasn't he an Ontario cabinet minister for a few years?"

"That's Dad. He got a team of lawyers and investigators on the case, and they soon discovered that the little fishing boat didn't have any navigation lights. Plus, the three girls, all locals, were underage and had been drinking at a high school party before the crash. Dad got my charges argued down to reckless endangerment with a suspended sentence, and I lost my driver's licence for six months and that was it, other than a headline in the *Toronto Sun*: "Bay Street Legal Whiz Gets Son Off In Boating Fatality." I accidentally killed a girl, and by that fall I was living in a Queen's University frat house with the rest of my life to look forward to. As soon as I graduated, I moved here to get away from the rumours, not that anyone seemed interested anymore. So that's who I am, Erin. That's who you're involved with. I should've told you sooner, but I couldn't. I couldn't because I knew what it might do to us. What it might make you think of me because you'd know I accidentally killed a girl."

While I was shocked, what I will always remember is how Robbie looked that night. Like a lost teenage boy. I hugged him and couldn't let go. He had risked everything to show me his most vulnerable self. Since that night we've only talked about it a couple of times. I know he and his family quietly donate money to a scholarship given out at the girl's high school in her honour.

As Robbie rose through the party's political circles, first as a researcher, later in communications, and finally as an EA, he was hopeful that he had outrun his past. By his late twenties he had begun to position himself for a run at an upcoming by-election nomination in a district that's adjacent to the one I now hold. Then he got outed.

The Halifax satire magazine *HFX Candid* came out with the story splashed across its front page in bold black letters. "BOAT DEATH IN EA'S PAST MAY SINK CANDIDACY." It played up how Robbie's dad weighed in and alleged he pulled in some favours to get his boy off. That's probably true. James Morrison would do anything for his eldest son, as I would for Zoey. Before I had her, I wasn't certain whether I would have chosen to protect my son the same way that James had. Now I know I wouldn't have blinked an eye.

The *HFX Candid* piece knocked my husband for a loop, especially because he knew the tip probably came from a source in our party who was backing someone else for the nomination. It slammed the door shut on elected politics for him—or at least Robbie was convinced it did. I didn't agree and some of his political buddies thought it could be overcome too, but Robbie didn't want to go through it.

So he decided to study law, choosing Dalhousie because it's a good school and we were already making a life in Halifax. Robbie's parents helped us buy a townhouse in Halifax's Fairview neighbourhood, and Mom and Dad helped us move in. After Robbie graduated, the premier tried to coax him back with a senior job in the PO. Robbie struggled with the decision yet knew it was time to walk away, especially when he got the articling offer at the most prestigious law firm in town.

Still, he's got the political virus in his blood. Years ago, he would've given anything to have my seat at the cabinet table. I understand his jealousy, but it makes me mad. He's not fully supporting me at a time when I need it. We'll have to work our way through this, like we've had to with other things. It's not going to be easy.

CHAPTER 16

"How'd you know I was a journalist for six years?"

"I overheard your colleagues talking outside the Red Room when you were sworn in to cabinet. What a pleasure to converse with a fellow journalist. I have always said there was no more invigorating opportunity to make one's way in the world than by bringing your countrymen news of Nova Scotia, the far-flung British Empire, or from our American cousins."

"My newspaper career pales compared to yours, Joe. My highlight was winning an Atlantic Journalism Award for a feature story on women's boxing. Dad was in the business as a reporter and copy editor at the *Chronicle* for thirty-five years. Mom taught biology."

"Did you say your father worked for a newspaper called the *Chronicle*? That was the name of the first newspaper I owned. James Spike and I purchased the *Weekly Chronicle* and promptly changed the name to the *Acadian*. Those were the days. I did not know what was what when I began, but my God it was exciting. Of course, later that year, I think it was December of '27, I took over the *Novascotian*, which was a whole different order of business with more subscribers and greater influence. A bit more sobering, that, yet still a delight. I introduced my own little innovations to our profession, such as coverage of the debates of the Legislature. When I first began, it was not seen as appropriate or, frankly, of interest. Through my own unique method, I was able to quickly transcribe the speeches. Of course, in my day there were no accommodations made for reporters in the House, no desks and such, and so I scribbled my notes by using my top hat as a writing table."

Joe is winding up like he does when he slips into story-telling mode. The light begins to dance in those blue eyes, and he becomes animated, his body telling the story as much as his voice.

"Why in only one year I built the circulation up to eight hundred subscribers, about half in Halifax and the rest spread across Nova Scotia from Glace Bay to Yarmouth, with a smattering in New Brunswick and the Canadas. In Halifax, my rivals were primarily the *Acadian*, the *Journal*, and the *Acadian Recorder*. Outside of Halifax, I had only one rival, Jotham Blanchard and his fellow scribblers at the *Colonial Patriot* in Pictou. And while Blanchard and I battled each other on the pages of our opposing newspapers numerous times in the early years, I must admit that the sickly and bespectacled fellow gave me my first education in liberal politics. He opened my eyes to show me the error of my ways."

Joe pauses and nods his head in agreement with his own words.

"So, we are both from newspaper families. My venerated father, John Senior, and my half-brother, John, were printers, and my father also wrote articles in his youth. It is not widely known, but Father wrote one of the first accounts of the Battle of Lexington and Concord during the American Revolution before he was forced to flee America."

"That's amazing. Your dad covered one of the most famous events in American history."

"Yes, it was the opening battle in the spring of 1775, and Father, a young man of twenty, witnessed all its splendid horror. Fifty colonials and about the same number of English troops killed. The next day he published a short article in the *Massachusetts Gazette* and in the *Boston Weekly News* followed by a broadsheet the following day. A few months later, Father witnessed the Battle of Bunker Hill where a great many of the King's troops lost their lives charging up the hill and capturing it. He wrote and printed a broadsheet describing that battle too. When I was a lad, he often told me the story of watching the English general as he led the final bayonet charge up the hill with bullets flying through the tails of his coat as he championed our forces to victory over the rebels."

"I can't say Dad covered any famous battles or political scandals, although he did interview Bobby Orr, Anne Murray, Zamfir, 'the Master of the Pan Flute,' and 'The Man They Call Raveen.'"

"Being a newspaperman was certainly a wonderful opportunity to converse with the leading men of the day in politics, science, and the healing arts. As an editor and publisher, through connections I even had the pleasure of a fine chat and good, invigorating walk on Chebucto Head with the English novelist Charles Dickens when he visited Halifax in '42 while on his way to America. One of the few men I ever met who was my match for energy. Have you heard mention of him?"

"He's well-known to this day as one of the greatest

writers in the English language. I recently read *Bleak House* for the first time, but my favourite is *A Tale of Two Cities.*"

"Sadly, I have not had the opportunity to read it. I leaned more toward *The Pickwick Papers*. While it was certainly delightful to talk with the leading men, some of my most joyous moments as a reporter were talking to fishermen, farmers, and small merchants on my many rambles through our homeland, particularly in the early days. More delightful, honest, and hospitable people one has never met. I learned more of life from these humble folk than I ever gleaned at the glittering tables of English manor houses or watching debates in the mother of parliaments in London."

"What do you miss most about the newspaper business?"

"Naturally I miss informing and shaping the public opinion of our fellow Nova Scotians on the issues of the day, be they on responsible government, the need to embrace railway development, or on the question of Confederation. On a more simple level, I miss the indescribable delight of seeing one's work in type on paper. I miss the smell of fresh ink upon a clean page as it comes off the presses. I ask you, Erin, is there a more wonderful, a more honest scent of one's hard work than that?"

"No, the smell of a freshly printed paper with your byline on a front-page story is pretty awesome. I miss talking with my colleagues in the newsroom just before the deadline pressure hits and you've got to write like a madwoman. All the morbid jokes and swapping tales about the real stories behind the headlines that are never going to make it into the newspaper for fear of libel or because there were still facts to be chased down."

"I understand you exactly. Tom Haliburton and a few of our friends met weekly at my home for years to trade gossip and humour at the expense of the humbugs and prigs who governed our homeland and ran its commerce. We called ourselves The Club. There was Dr. Grigor, the good Scottish general practitioner; the lawyer and future politician Larry O'Connor Doyle; and Captain Kincaid. All witty fellows. What joyous times we had. By the end of the night, one would be exhausted from laughing so hard, and my hand would be sore from ferociously scribbling it all down. Oh, the silly songs and snatches of verse from our readings that we would trade.

'We'll drink to-night with hearts as light,
To loves as gay and fleeting
As bubbles that swim, on the beaker's brim,
And break on the lips while meeting.'

"For a few years these fellows supplied the *Novascotian* with witticisms and satire that lampooned the foolishness of our day and the actions of some of our public men. Naturally, The Club's contributions were anonymous and poked fun in a way that was so good-natured and witty that it was difficult for the targeted fellows to publicly take offence."

Joe's large face is as guileless as a child's, emotions flashing across it like images on a movie screen. Humour is currently playing, from his youthful grin to his smiling eyes.

"These articles made my newspaper more entertaining and less dependent on stories grabbed from English and American newspapers or from the Canadas. In my day, we editors robbed articles from newspapers outside of our region like bold highwaymen. Stories on English politics or European affairs, the doctrine of Buddhism or the best way to grow potatoes or brew homemade beer were the backbone of my newspaper. From time to time I would even publish excerpts of novels from the great writers of the day, such as Sir Walter Scott and Dickens, of course. I made certain the *Novascotian* included the poems of Samuel Taylor Coleridge too, as he is unparalleled."

"Interesting. Your paper had elements in it, like poems and excerpts from fiction, that are usually only found in magazines now."

"Tom's character Sam Slick took shape in the *Novascotian*. Indeed, The Club was active a few years before Tom struck out on his own. Did you know that I published the first edition of Tom's book *The Clockmaker* that not only made him famous in Nova Scotia and the Canadas, but also the toast of London?"

"I think I read something about it."

"Why in 1837 a pirated version of *The Clockmaker* published in London rivalled Dickens's new novel *The Pickwick Papers* in popularity. The unfortunate story of how that pirated edition came to be and its financial injury to me is for us to discuss another time. You know, Tom tried to dissuade me from leaving journalism and entering politics. He thought I had far more to offer our country as a reporter and editor than as a Member of the Legislative Assembly. I am not certain, though, that he did not fear the increasing reform bent of my public opinions and worried what I might achieve in the political arena, for he was lifelong Tory. He sent me a lovely letter on the matter that ended with a splendid line: 'I say no more, you will readily see the friend, if I'm mistaken in this view, for real friends only differ from us in our favourite projects.'"

"So meetings of The Club are what you miss most about journalism?"

"Those evenings burn bright in my memory. Even so, I must say I found my greatest personal reward in the many Sunday evenings I devoted to the further education of my apprentices, fine lads all. The opportunity to shape their young minds with readings and discussions in front of my own hearth, with Susan Ann graciously providing endless cups of tea and delicious cakes, gave me no end of satisfaction. As a self-educated man I felt a responsibility to aid fellows who, like me, had not had the opportunities afforded by a formal education. I could not be prouder than to say that four of these fellows moved on to leading positions at Maritime newspapers, while one of their colleagues, Richard Nugent, eventually took over the *Novascotian*. And then of course there was Ennis, my most devoted supporter and loyal aide, whom I believe you have met."

"Yes, recently. A lovely man."

"Indeed, like a son to me and a fine newspaperman."

"Joe, there's something else I've been wanting to ask you, if you don't mind. What's the afterlife like?

"Rather underwhelming, really. Rattling around Province House with little else to see or do but watch decade after decade of politicians come and go, promising careers flame and then burn out. An endless cycle of debating the same issues with minor variations on the theme. Our politicians never quite overcome the obstacles in the way of Nova Scotia's potential. Deals are struck, accommodations made —the endless detours around critical issues to avoid facing them head-on in a manly fashion."

"So what's it like to be a ghost?"

"Very limiting, I'm afraid. Ennis and I can flit about Province House like barn swallows, listening in to whatever conversations we please without being observed. Some people sense us but, unlike you, do not see us. I cannot eat or drink, I cannot see outside the windows of this place to glimpse what developments may have taken place in my native home. I cannot venture out of doors. Oh, how I yearn to hear a breeze tickling the leaves of a birch tree or smell salty ocean air. I cannot even converse with you about the weather, for I have no way of knowing what it is like outside."

"It's one of those otherworldly Halifax days, Joe, where only the tops of the harbour bridges peek out of the fog cloaking the harbour and the city."

"I have never had sight of either of the two bridges, still I can imagine the scene you paint from my journeys to England, where old London Bridge always poked its renowned head out of the fog that shrouded that colossus of a city."

"It doesn't sound like this afterlife would be very stimulating for a man like yourself who lived such an active life."

"Indeed, that frames it exactly. It is not stimulating. Ennis does what he can, God bless him, to keep me amused and engaged, but it grows tiring. It gives one a vast amount of time to reflect on one's life, the victories and defeats, and the regrets. Perhaps far too much time. As always, our conversation has been stimulating, nonetheless I am tired and must retire for the day. Not to sleep, mind you—another limitation of this afterlife—only to nap in a most unsatisfying way. I have battled insomnia for 150 years, and it is a wearying struggle. Erin, my best wishes to you in your cabinet endeavours, and I wish you every success in this next step up the political ladder. I caution you that the higher one climbs, the shakier the ladder becomes."

CHAPTER 17

"Why, I had a wonderful childhood, Erin, idyllic really. I was a wild boy, spending my days fishing, swimming, and rowing on the Northwest Arm or dashing through the underbrush in search of small game. I returned to our modest cottage for supper, mud-smeared, brambles knitted to my clothing, and fell into the loving arms of my grown-up half-sister, Jane, and my beloved father."

We are talking in the Red Chamber, the second largest room in Province House, the size of an elementary school gym. Its high, white ceilings, eleven large windows, and ornate, white plaster mouldings give the room the sunny richness of an English manor house ballroom.

I don't have enough time for my work as a minister or an MLA, let alone for Robbie and Zoey, yet I find myself making time to talk to Joe. I'm not sure how relevant his bits of advice and stories are to my life, but I always have a smile on my face afterward, like I've just taken a candlelit bath with a glass of Pinot Grigio.

"You lived like one of Peter Pan's Lost Boys. Didn't you have to go to school?"

"I did attend from time to time, but it was more than two miles away, and Father was perhaps too indulgent of me, being the last of his children. He was fifty years old when I was born. Through much of my early life I had three great teachers: my honourable father, the Bible, and Shakespeare. Not a morning went by that I did not rise to find my father already in his usual chair in the kitchen reading the Good Book. My early education was as fine as any young fellow received, based on Father's reading and his abiding faith in God. 'Like as a star, that maketh not haste; that taketh not rest, let each be fulfilling his God-given best,' he told me, time and again. And what of your childhood, Erin?"

"Comfortable and loving with two supportive parents who found the right balance between strictness and freedom, considering I was an only child. Plenty of soccer and piano lessons and the debate team when I was in high school. Lots of hanging with my best friend, Summer."

"I had only a few friends as a boy, but I met other youths my age when I joined my half-brother, John, in our family's printing business. He needed the help, and frankly I needed the rigour and structure of a young apprentice's life."

"How old were you when you went to work?"

"I was thirteen. I was a robust, burly lad and threw myself into the physical and mental challenges of a print shop. Unlike many of my fellow apprentices, I took time to read the papers and documents that our shop produced as the Queen's Printer. Reading complicated issues upside down, as a printer is wont to do on the job, does a great deal to increase one's mental faculties."

"That's awfully young to be out in the working world. Was it unusual?"

"At that time it was normal. Perhaps not for people like Tom Haliburton and others on the treadmill toward a formal education at King's College in Windsor, but not unusual in Halifax with its thriving commercial enterprises in need of young fellows."

On a nearby wall hangs a portrait of Haliburton, Howe's long-time friend who became a provincial court judge after serving in the Nova Scotia Legislature.

"At the end of the day I would throw off my stained printer's apron and dive into Halifax Harbour for a refreshing dip, at least in the spring and summer months. There is nothing quite like floating in the inky black harbour, looking toward the fortifications on Georges Island as the dusk paints their outlines. Afterward, I walked home and read by candlelight for hours on end, everything I could get my hands on. And that is how I spent my early teens, working with John, studying on my own, conversing with my venerable father, and sharing my future plans with my dearest sister, Jane. Like all of Halifax, on summer nights I turned out to hear the Regimental Band play and on Sundays watched the garrison parade to St. Paul's for service, dressed in their brightest frippery. Not that I necessarily attended church regularly myself, for I have always been somewhat uncommitted in that regard."

We are sitting at the Cornwallis table, brought to Nova Scotia during the founding of Halifax in 1749 by Lord Cornwallis aboard the HMS *Beaufort*. Later, likely at this table, Cornwallis signed the infamous Scalping Proclamation, which offered a bounty for every Mi'kmaq adult or child that was killed.

"My first brush with any sort of recognition came when I entered a poetry contest sponsored by our Lieutenant-Governor, the Earl of Dalhousie. He felt my poem about

Melville Island and the old prison there showed great promise for one so young. Of course, I had grown up near the island, which sits only a quarter mile across the Northwest Arm from my childhood home. I looked upon it often from my favourite perch on a mossy stone wall."

"A poem about an old prison. Interesting choice for a boy. Do you remember any of it?"

As I look across the table, Joe is framed by eight-foot tall portraits of King George III and Queen Charlotte on the far wall behind two plush, yellow throne chairs.

"It's been more than two hundred years, yet I think I can recall snippets of the beginning:

'Record of War, behold you little Isle,

Whose brow is crown'd by many a mouldering pile,

...something, something...where groups of buildings sinking to decay...

Throw their dark shadows o'er the narrow bay...

...with a mirror's smoothness, brightly shines

While the last ray of summer's sun reclines

Upon its placid breast—where...blue sky,

And blended rocks, and groves, reflected lie...'

"I am sorry, Erin, it has been a great while. Regardless, the Lieutenant-Governor invited me to visit him at Government House, where he praised my work and had my name registered for any future invitations to state balls and dinners. You know, I continued to write poetry all my life, with limited recognition, yet it did not matter. Poetry always restored my soul. Poetry was the maiden I loved; politics was the harridan I married."

"I must look for more of your poetry."

"Our conversation has stirred up splendid memories for me. Oh, to see my boyhood home again, surrounded by oaks and our little garden with the fragrance of apple and cherry trees on the salty breeze. Our little world of sun, wind, and water, separated from the rest of humanity by a sacred grove of pines. I would pay every pound I ever earned to spend an hour in that wondrous paradise.

'Midst Trees, and Birds, and Summer Flowers
Those fleeting years went by;
With sports and books and joyous hours,
Like lightning seemed to fly.

'THE ROD, the Gun, the Spear, the Oar,
I plied by Lake and Sea—
Happy to swim from shore to shore,
Or rove the Woodlands free.'"

The poet Joe Howe. Who knew? And yet poetry was clearly his one true love besides Susan Ann. His face gets dreamy and looks twenty years younger when he recites his lines. A hidden talent of his, or least forgotten to most people today.

I've come to realize that everyone has a hidden talent, hopefully not so buried that it's hidden from themselves. I might even have one. It may be time to take another look at the collection of short stories I began years ago and never finished. My conversation with Joe opens that closed door, if only a crack.

CHAPTER 18

The Department of Health Promotion's programs are beginning to make sense to me. I'm far from comfortable with all the details, but as I reread various briefing notes, more of it seems familiar. I'm losing that lost-at-sea feeling. More importantly, my relationship with my deputy, Margaret Cameron, is growing. As I learn more about being a cabinet minister, I'm discovering how important that relationship is to my being able to achieve anything.

A good deputy minister positions your initiatives for success at cabinet or treasury board, a subcommittee of cabinet that controls the purse strings. She socializes other ministers and her fellow deputies at other departments to the initiatives your department proposes. Since few files or issues rest with only one government department these days, getting cooperation and support from other departments is critical.

The turning point in our relationship happened last week when I did something that is apparently rare: I asked her advice on what we might want to achieve during my time as minister. Normally either the governing party's election platform or the premier's mandate letter to each minister sets out what Government wants done in each department's area of responsibility. In my case, the department is such a low priority that these contain nothing of significance.

I had no professional experience in the field of health promotion prior to being appointed minister. If I'd had a choice of cabinet assignments, I would've preferred Minister Responsible for the Advisory Council on the Status of Women or maybe Minister of Municipal Affairs. I've always tried to exercise and maintain a good diet and played varsity soccer at King's College, but I have no burning passion to achieve anything specific as Minister of Health Promotion. As I get a better understanding of our department's role, though, I can see possibilities.

"Margaret, I hope you don't mind me saying this, but now that I've read about our mandate and gone through the briefing book on what projects and programs we have underway, I've got to say it doesn't seem very ambitious."

While I waited for her answer, I glanced over at a nearby bulletin board that's crammed with Zoey's drawings and daycare art projects.

"It might not be as ambitious as it could be, Minister, but there are some solid programs and initiatives," she said, then hesitated. "Is there something in particular you were hoping to achieve, some initiative or capital expenditure?"

The way she asked I could tell she was waiting for me to suggest something politically motivated like she had been asked to do too many times before by either past ministers or the Premier's Office or both. Her question had a "here we go again" tone.

"Frankly, I don't know enough yet about what we do to come up with anything that's more than half-baked; still, I do get the sense that given the expertise of our staff and the needs across the province that we could do more, couldn't we? Or are we handcuffed by the size of the department's budget?"

"No, we have a decent budget that could always be reallocated to support new, modest initiatives or programs. Something big would require an ask of the treasury board though, which isn't easy."

"Let's say you were sitting in my chair and had the opportunity to bring something forward, what would you do?"

Again, she paused and looked at me as if I might be setting a trap.

"Minister, if you're asking my opinion, I think Government might be a bit more ambitious for our department. For somewhere between $200,000 and half a million each, there's a couple of programs we could propose that could really help. Not to change the world, but to make a difference for some people."

It was like opening a shaken bottle of Perrier. Margaret's fair complexion flushed as she became animated. For the next half-hour she spewed out the details of two potential programs and what she believed they could accomplish.

One program would send nutritionists into communities to put on healthy eating clinics. Margaret said research had found that people who want to make healthy eating choices don't always have enough hands-on information about healthier cooking techniques and what to buy to improve their nutrition. The other would send physical trainers into communities to put on workshops to help people choose an activity or hobby that might best suite their lifestyle and health needs.

The broad outlines of both programs had already been written and the expenses costed a few years ago, but the minister of the day hadn't pursued them because the Premier's Office wasn't interested.

"They sound a helluva lot better and more useful than most of the stuff in my briefing notes. And you think they could make a difference, both in urban and rural Nova Scotia?"

"I do, Minister. We've done the research. It shows they could be successful with a very modest investment, at least by government standards."

"I'm game. If I'm going to put in all this time being a cabinet minister, then I want to do something useful for people, not just sit here and hope I don't screw up while I wait for a bigger cabinet post."

Margaret, who normally plays her cards carefully, had a smile on her face.

"I'll assign some staff to begin working on them this week. You won't regret it, Minister. I think those programs can do some real good if we can get the Premier's Office to greenlight them. Of course, Dunc McDonald may not be happy. One of the programs overlaps with some of his department's responsibilities, and Dunc can be very territorial."

"We'll deal with that if it comes up. So that's that. Hey, have we hired some new senior people recently? I've seen two or three faces in the office that I haven't seen before, and none of them are kids."

"We filled a couple of vacant positions with some good senior staff from another department that became available."

"That's great, Margaret. It sounds like a win for us."

"Just call me Margie. Everyone who doesn't work for me calls me Margie."

THE RED CHAMBER is beautifully decorated for the Speaker's Christmas party for MLAs, their spouses, and house staff. Green wreaths of garland adorned with red ribbons are draped above the ivory-white double doors, which frame a twinkling Christmas tree inside. The light in the brass chandeliers is turned down low, like the soft gaslight that long illuminated the room. In the corner a pianist plays "All Through the Night" and "White Christmas" on a century-old piano, tugging on nostalgia's heartstrings.

The voices are loud and cheerful at this rare social gathering of the three parties. Robbie circulates easily among the crowd and knows most people on both sides of the aisle. I share a quick chat and hug with Nathalie Amirault and Grace Smith and some laughs with Doug Brayfield before moving along. It's a room full of expert socializers who float around like dancers at a Viennese ball. LeBlanc is being proudly paraded about by her balding, sixty-something husband, one of the wealthiest men in the province and a big financial backer of our party. Dunc makes his way through the sea of people like a frigate at full steam, his tiny, frowning wife trailing in his wake. I exchange season's greetings with some Opposition politicians I hardly know.

"So what do you do for celebrations at home?" I ask Anna Mae Denny, a Cape Bretoner and the Legislature's first and only Mi'kmaw MLA.

Anna Mae is one of the few people of colour at this gath-

ering and one of less than a handful in the Nova Scotia
Legislature, which is a profoundly white, male space.

"Nothing much different than everyone else. I'm from a
big Catholic family, and so we all go to midnight mass and
then over to Mom's for a big feed before heading home.
Maybe there's different dishes served than you'd have, a
good moose roast and maybe some lushinikn, our version of
fry bread, and then a few hours of sleep before the kids get
us up."

"I hope you have a lovely Christmas and a good break
from this place. God knows we all need it," I say before we
exchange the awkward hug of strangers.

"Etawey Wli-Nipi-Alasutman, to you and your family.
That's Merry Christmas. And Pusu'l Puna'ne. Happy New
Year, Erin."

Anna Mae is a trailblazer, a former school principal and
community activist. It's too bad she's not part of our Government instead of a member of the Third Party. Her presence
here is a sign of the gradual evolution of Nova Scotia as we
all move very slowly through the reconciliation process.

She's one of seventeen women in this House of fifty-one
MLAs; nearly half of the women serve in our caucus. In
some ways, I have more in common politically with Anna
Mae and her leader, Shauntay Downey, the first African
Nova Scotian to head a party, than I do with most women
serving in our Government or in the Official Opposition.

Some of my female colleagues are hardly feminists,
with many of the women my age less aware than they
should be of the long struggle for equality in politics.
Women only gained the right to run in Nova Scotia elections in 1918. It took forty-two years and eight unsuccessful
female candidates before Gladys Muriel Porter won an election in 1960 to represent Kings North. It took another

twenty-five years before the appointment of a woman to cabinet.

Some of the older female MLAs are of a generation that had to play politics in an overly aggressive, elbows out, male way in order to succeed in what was—and still is—a man's game. Women like Janet Zwicker are far from being allies of their fellow female MLAs, especially younger ones.

In the midst of the social swirl, I sneak downstairs, past the security guards, throwing a quick "I've got to take a call in private" over my shoulder before heading into the Veterans Room and turning on the lights. Joe arrives in short order.

"Why, Erin, you look beautiful in your evening gown. Quite lovely. Reminds me of all the beautiful young women who attended the Navy balls at Admiralty House when the British fleet was in town for the summer. Your Robbie is the luckiest man in Province House tonight."

"Thanks, Joe. We're upstairs at the Christmas party, and while I was here I thought I'd pop by with something for you and Ennis."

I take two small gifts out of my purse, one wrapped in shiny gold paper, the other in silver. With childish delight, Joe rips the paper off the gift I hand him and stares down at a copy of *A Tale of Two Cities*. Tears well up in his eyes.

"I do not know what to say. I am quite overcome. I have not received a gift in a very long time. This novel is by my old companion, Mr. Dickens. Delightful. I have practically read through the thousands of books in the Legislative Library. But I feel rather guilty, as I have nothing for you."

"You give me the gift of your wisdom every time we talk. I have something for Ennis too. Where is he?"

"Regrettably, he is indisposed, but nothing serious. I will ensure that he gets it."

"It's cigars. A friend of mine told me they were quite good ones."

"You have no idea how pleased he will be. On behalf of the two of us, I wish you all the compliments of the season. A Merry Christmas to you and yours, Erin, and God Save the Queen."

"And the same to you and to Ennis."

CHAPTER 19

"You must've covered every kilometre of Nova Scotia on your western and eastern rambles, Joe. I was reading about them in one of Dad's books. You probably saw more of this province than anyone before or since."

It's my first visit to Province House in the new year. I slipped into the Legislative Library a few minutes ago with another lame excuse. The security guards are so used to me coming by, even after hours like this, that they don't say much, but I know it's arousing curiosity.

"I cannot speak to your presumption about my travels as compared with others, although I do admit to covering vast reaches of our homeland many times over, particularly in the early years at the *Novascotian*, when I was trying to sign up new subscribers in the countryside. I saw a great deal of our country from '28 to about '35, and it was delightful. To make a success of my newspaper I had no choice but to canvass outside of Halifax for subscribers. In those days, the city only had about 14,000 souls out of the 140,000 living in

Nova Scotia, which were interspersed amongst large stretches of unbroken wilderness. Windsor, Lunenburg, Pictou, Yarmouth, and Truro were only modest villages. Kentville had only the delightful Stage Coach Inn and thirty houses, and Bridgewater was a tiny settlement. Why there was only one bookshop outside of Halifax, James Dawson's in Pictou, which was also a printer."

"Back then, some of Nova Scotia must've still been in its natural state. Almost like in pre-contact times when it was Mi'kma'ki and only the Mi'kmaq called it home."

"Indeed. Breathtakingly beautiful. Naturally, some of these rambles were more successful than others, both in gathering subscribers and finding new subjects to report to my readers. On one trip in the fall of '29 I signed up forty-three new subscribers in only six weeks on the road. However, other rambles were less successful. I remember one June day in Guysborough County riding thirty miles and paddling a few miles downriver by canoe, and at the end of the day I had not one new subscriber or one sou in collections. On another occasion, I was in Annapolis Royal and realized that on the opposite bank of the Annapolis River, in Granville Ferry, I had a subscriber who was a number of years in arrears."

As Joe launches into his tale, a grin begins at the corner of his blue eyes, a now familiar sign that he's about to dip into his bag of stories.

"I asked for my subscriber's whereabouts and was told where the wealthy farmer lived. I crossed on the ferry, quickly found the man, and pointed out his debt in my book. 'Certainly, the account has run up too high,' he replied to me. 'I will go and fetch the money. You sit and wait here, young mister, on this comfortable log, until I return.' The man proceeded to walk to a house a distance off, but in full view of myself. The last I saw of him was his back as he closed the door to the home. I remained seated on the log, expecting the man to open his door at any moment and trudge back to where I sat with his money purse in hand. After nearly an hour's wait it dawned on me that he had no intention whatsoever of returning. I headed back to Annapolis Royal no wealthier, but certainly wiser."

"That's too funny. Today, we'd say that you got played."

"Oh yes, indeed, I got played. I got played," he says, chuckling at the phrase.

"For the most part I enjoyed the physical aspect of my travels," he continues, "the whispers of our great forests and the thrum of the ocean lapping our fine shores. Still, it was never easy. In those days we had only two coach roads—the Western Road, from Halifax to Windsor and through the Annapolis Valley to Annapolis Royal, and the Eastern Road, from Halifax to Truro and on to Pictou. All other roads were no more than paths broken by the Mi'kmaq, good only for horses or carts. I recall travelling through Cape Breton in July of 1830 through incessant rain, where the mud was up to my horse's knees and sometimes up to his haunches. Another time I was travelling in the fall and ended up having to camp out rough in the woods for the night. Why, it was so cold that I put on every piece of clothing in my saddlebag. I was stiff as a board by morning. On more than one occasion, I resorted to using shank's pony for my travels when no horse or coach was available to me."

"Shank's pony?"

"My own two good feet, Erin."

I laugh, then say, "I read that sometimes your rambles kept you away for almost six months. Didn't your trip in 1829 take you far away, to Saint John, Boston, and New York?

How did you manage to get your newspaper out while you were away for such long stretches?"

"I had Susie, my own little editor, and my fine apprentices to thank for the *Novascotian* surviving such times. My darling wife had newspaper ink pumping through her veins. We kept in frequent touch through the post while I was on my rambles. I would tell her my upcoming travel itinerary and where I planned to stay, and she would send along letters and copies of the newspaper for me to peruse. In turn, I would send subscription collections and my stories back to her as well as criticisms, suggestions, and bons mots on the state of the newspaper. Naturally, I would also send her the loving words that one sends one's spouse when you are long parted, but those are too personal to speak of."

"Joe, your rambles must've been very hard on Susan Ann, left at home to look after the newspaper, the kids, and your business affairs while you travelled about for weeks on end, free as a bird. Few wives or partners would stand for it these days."

"Perhaps you have a point. Admittedly, it was a different time where men and women had a perspective on the responsibilities of marriage that you might find unacceptable today. In retrospect I should have been more thoughtful of the burden I placed on dearest Susie."

"Tell me more about your rambles."

"I count two blessings from my rambles: getting to know my fellow Nova Scotians, and seeing the most beautiful countryside in all the British Empire. I talked with my countrymen in the fragrant orchards of the Annapolis Valley, on fishing stages in Lunenburg, on modest farms in Cumberland County, and after Catholic mass with Abbé Sigogne at Pointe-de-l'Église. I met with one subscriber on Lochaber Lake who had plastered the walls of his cottage with the

Novascotian. I broke bread at their modest tables, kissed the cheeks of their charming wives, and bounced their babies on my knees."

Joe's fondness for kissing nearly every woman he met often led to questions from political enemies about his fidelity to Susan Ann. It would be totally unacceptable today. When I recently asked Ennis about it, he dismissed it as a sign of Joe's good nature.

"Despite all the dark rumours about Joe having an illegitimate child in every village, all I can say is that while Joe loved the social company of all women, he only loved one woman, his dearest Susan Ann," he had assured me.

Joe continues. "I told our rural countrymen stories and jokes and brought them news of Halifax, which was like another world to them. I drank tea with their grandparents and danced at their children's weddings. No man was greater blessed than I. When I stood for politics my relations with these fine people held me in good stead, nonetheless that was through no intent or grand plan on my part. And if I had never taken to the political stage, I would have still considered the opportunity to meet so many simple and honest people to be one of my life's greatest rewards."

"I've got to say, Joe, the combination of your being a native Haligonian and your rambles gave you a sense of Nova Scotia that's unmatched by today's politicians. I can't think of any of my fellow cabinet ministers who understand all of the province. The city ministers know Halifax and the rural ministers know how their own counties tick, but it seems no one has a thorough sense of the whole."

"As I said, Erin, it was through no plan on my part. My ramblings gave me the immeasurable benefit of seeing the beauty of our fair countryside. Can anywhere surpass it? I think not. I remember one ramble in particular that took me through the beautiful Annapolis Valley."

"My husband and I love the Valley. Beautiful countryside, great food, good coffee, fun winery tours, and some killer microbreweries."

"You should be enamoured of it. I can still recall what I wrote in my newspaper after that wonderous afternoon: 'Around you, the eternal hills are piled up, as though they were intended as a barrier to protect the fertility they enclose, and beyond is the Minas Basin, with its islands resting like ornaments on its bosom, and old Blomidon flinging his stern shadow upon its waves.'"

"That's beautiful, Joe."

"I took so much solace in the bosom of nature during my travels. It gave me the opportunity to reflect on the public issues of the day and on my own philosophy in the silences between the breezes. The Nova Scotia countryside was my church and did far more to renew my spirits and lift my soul than any dry Anglican sermon ever did. Paul the Apostle had his epiphany on the road to Damascus. I had mine while travelling by pony on the road to Lunenburg. There was a bright sun, a clear sky, and birdsong everywhere. My heart overflowed with the goodness and mercy of He who created us. It was perfection, save that I did not have Susan by my side. Why, I thought of more poetry on that day in the saddle than I could write in a month. At the end of the day, I sat down to a bounteous repast at John Lennox's inn followed by a fine cigar outside in the evening air. It may have been one of the most satisfying days of my life."

"Like most Haligonians, I haven't seen a lot of Nova Scotia. It seems that if you don't come from some other part of the province or have relatives living outside the city, you never get around to seeing much of this place."

"It is a misfortune that I am certain can be easily corrected with all the various means of transportation that one has today. I trust you will make amends, Erin. I assure you that travelling through our Nova Scotia will provide you with greater nourishment than one would receive at the finest dining establishments in this fair city."

CHAPTER 20

I'm embarrassed by what happened yesterday and what it says about who I'm becoming as a politician and as a person. Nathalie Amirault and I decided to get together for a quick drink late in the afternoon and headed to The Old Triangle. Instead of our usual table in The Snug, we found a booth in the corner for privacy. We'd been dying to talk about life as cabinet newbies. We've had quick huddles after cabinet, and I've seen Nathalie rolls her eyes more than once at meetings, but we've been so busy we haven't had time to catch up.

"Erin, it blows me away how things work," Nathalie said halfway through her second glass of Pinot Noir. "Look at what we approved at cabinet this morning. Our big economic development strategy, that agriculture thing, the cultural initiative, and what took the most time? A wedge issue, designed to alienate the Official Opposition's supporters, that everyone knows will do absolutely nothing useful for anyone but will force their party to publicly take an unpopular position. That's what everyone focused on."

"I hear you. The political shit drives me."

Nathalie looked tired, although no more than me with my racoon eyes that I try to hide under makeup.

"We spent all of ten minutes discussing our economic development strategy. I think it's going to be great, but of course I'm the Minister of Economic Development. And I know the folks at the department have been working on it for over a year and think it's solid, still there were virtually no questions. It's a big chunk of funding. My department could be out to lunch on its economic projections. No one challenged the proposal or our numbers."

"And the only question you got was from Janet Zwicker asking why you didn't consider her Bridgewater district more instead of Cape Breton."

"Exactly. She didn't care whether the strategy would work in the long term or not. She only wanted the gravy to be doled out in her district, not somewhere else. The short-sightedness is so frustrating. I don't think most of our colleagues read the briefing papers on the agenda items before they come to the table. All the stuff we talked about when we were backbenchers is there in spades. We drift from issue to issue with no overall plan or direction on where we want to take the province. We make isolated polit-ical decisions, one at a time."

"Of course, Nathalie, governing is way more complicated than we imagined. All the steps you have to take to get stuff through the bureaucratic process, to get financial support from treasury board, and then to get onto the cabinet agenda. My God, who knew? The turnaround time to get something done is forever. Even on simple stuff."

"That's true. How have your staff been?"

"Pretty good. I've been impressed. Most of the senior people are smart and hardworking. Margie, my DM, has been really helpful. I've got a lot of time for her. She's super

bright and genuinely wants to get things done. And the
Premier's Office has finally assigned me an executive
assistant, an Antigonish County girl, Mackenzie Chisholm,
who's been working in the caucus office. She's only twenty-
four and almost fresh out of St. FX. I don't really know her,
still she seems bright and eager. How about you?"

"My deputy, Charmaine, is smart too. Pretty reasonable
to work with. She's a real player though. I get the sense that
everything she does is to position herself to advance. If it
doesn't gain her favour with the premier or Premier's Office,
she wants no part of it. She wants to be the DM of the Office
of the Premier, the deputy of all deputies, and she wants it
yesterday. By the way, she mentioned something that I
thought you should know. Apparently, Dunc has been a real
prick to some of his senior departmental staff, and because
they're not unionized a handful have either left or been
forced out. No one has seen anything like it in years. The
Public Service Commission has been quietly scouting
around for places for these people to land, and your DM has
offered sanctuary and hired some. Charmaine only
mentioned it to say that she isn't getting involved because
she doesn't want to get on the wrong side of Dunc."

I found the news disappointing. I thought Margie knew
me well enough to let me in on what's going on. I guess she
needs to be careful too. That Dunc the Dick has struck again
didn't surprise me in the least.

"The thing I find the most shocking is how much power
LeBlanc and the folks in the Premier's Office have. The
premier listens to her and her people more than he listens
to his cabinet ministers, even senior ones like Janet. He's
wrapped around LeBlanc's finger."

"She's a powerful woman, Erin. Be careful around her.
I've seen enough of her kind in corporate boardrooms to

know to keep my guard up, although few of them dress as well as she does. LeBlanc does have awesome taste in clothes. There's no Frenchys shopping for that girl."

"It's not just LeBlanc. Most of the senior staff at the Premier's Office give off that same vibe of being confident that they're the smartest, most in-the-know people in the room. It's like no problem, or its solution, exists until they turn their minds to it. Yet sometimes they make the most arbitrary and ill-informed decisions imaginable and almost always at the last minute. When the shit hits the fan, as it does with rash decisions, they look to blame someone else, it's never their mistake."

"And they're so vindictive about doling out the blame, especially to our fellow cabinet ministers and caucus members. They're uglier to our own than to the Opposition."

"One last thing, Nathalie, and then no more work talk. But I've got to say that if I hear another comfortable, middle-class white guy around the cabinet table explain why we can't afford more money to support affordable housing or to tackle food insecurity, I'm going to throw up."

Nathalie was nodding along in agreement and about to add something when Doug Brayfield walked past our booth and popped his head in.

"Hey, gang, did I miss the email? If I did, sorry."

"We bumped into each other and decided to grab a quick one at the end of the day," I heard myself say. "Sit down. How goes it?"

"Good, not as busy as you two, I imagine, but keeping occupied. The past couple of months must have flown by for you guys. I've only seen you at caucus."

"It's been pretty hectic. I've had to shepherd a couple of

big economic initiatives through cabinet, so it's kept me pretty busy."

"So what's coming out next, Nathalie?"

"Can't really talk about it yet, Doug, not until I bring it to caucus."

"No, of course. I understand," he said, unable to hide his disappointment.

We chatted about this and that for ten uncomfortable minutes. How his wife was doing, how Zoey was doing, about a new guy Nathalie is seeing, as we all studiously avoided politics. Since Nathalie and I are in cabinet, we can't talk freely about politics with Doug anymore. We insist we should all get together soon, but none of us expects it to happen. A wall has come up between the two of us and Doug over a passion we once shared. The Three Musketeers are down to two. It makes me feel sad and guilty.

"Doug's a big boy, he understands cabinet confidentiality," Robbie said at home that night. "In any workplace there are senior people and junior people, and the fact is that senior people can't share everything with everyone. The senior partners at our firm don't tell us worker bees squat. That's the way it is."

He hugged me for a good long time afterward. We spooned in bed until I fell into a crappy sleep.

CHAPTER 21

It's five thirty, everyone has gone home, and the Legislative Library is empty as I snap on a table reading lamp. I haven't seen Joe in weeks. We're ramping up for the spring sitting of the Legislature, and I'm in endless rounds of briefings in preparation for Question Period and for legislation we're bringing forward.

I've got to be more careful about how often I use the library and the meeting rooms. Someone at Province House must've said something to the Premier's Office, because they asked whether there was a problem with my ministerial office space, adding that if there was, it could be renovated.

"There's no need for you to be over at the drafty House this time of year," the PO's staffer said, with the implication being to stay out of the Legislature staff's hair when the House isn't sitting.

My feet are turning cold, as though I stepped in a snowbank without boots, and the aroma of cigars is in the air. I look around, expecting to see Ennis Douglas. Then the taste of metal touches my tongue and my heart beats a bodhran's rhythm, which normally signals Joe's arrival.

My confusion clears when both Joe and Ennis appear beside a bust of young Queen Victoria. I've never seen them together. They materialize in the midst of a lively conversation and are smiling like Cheshire cats. Joe's eyes twinkle and Ennis has a liveliness I've never seen as he gently touches the older man's arm to make a point.

"Lovely to see you again, Erin. Our apologies for appearing in the midst of conversation. Ennis and I were having a lovely reminiscence about a foolish incident back in 1840, which thankfully turned out for the best."

"Joe is referring to a duel he fought that spring against John C. Halliburton, the s-s-son of Sir Brenton Halliburton."

"Wait a second, you fought a duel against Brenton Halliburton's son? Wasn't he the judge at your libel trial?"

"Yes, it was a few years after the trial. It was such a foolish affair that to this day neither of us is certain which words of mine about his pater caused young Halliburton to take such umbrage. It was certainly something I said during debate in the House in the spring of 1840; however, I said a great deal in those days against those few who ran our country so poorly. Frankly, it was impossible to refer to political abuse and not comment on it without striking someone."

"As best we can remember, it may have had to do with Joe saying that the large stipends that the judiciary received were not deserved. Either that or some comparison he made between Judge Halliburton and the *Novascotian*'s apprentices, which young Halliburton found to be uncouth and injurious to his father."

"Regardless, I found myself challenged by a young gentleman of the elite families whose challenge could not be ignored if I was to carry on as a credible public man. I had avoided a couple of other challenges previously; however, this one could not be dismissed."

"Joe, you could have been killed or killed him."

"Make no mistake, Erin, I detest duelling. A remnant of a barbarous age, it was slowly fading away and yet had not disappeared. It was the refuge of villains and the scourge of good men. I struggled with whether to accept his challenge, yet I knew in my heart of hearts that all my efforts would be for naught if Howe, the Great Reformer, were to be found a coward. Before the appointed morning, I wrote four letters that I left with my second, two addressed to my colleagues at the *Novascotian*, one to the people of Nova Scotia telling them I had no choice but to hazard my life rather than blight all my future prospects of being useful, and one to my lovely Susan Ann."

"What did you tell your wife?"

"They were the loving words that a man shares only with his wife. They are of a private and intimate nature. Let me just say, I told my cherished that she had always had my boyish heart, from the first time ever I saw her. Also, that thoughts of her and our young babes almost unmanned me and made me consider declining the challenge."

"She must've been incredibly worried. If Robbie ever tried something like that, I'd kill him first."

"No doubt, no doubt. And so, on a bright, crisp March morning in 1840, I and Herbert Huntington, my second and fellow Reformer, arrived at the assigned location, a clearing near the Martello Tower in Point Pleasant Park, for my duel with John C. Halliburton. I was thirty-six years old and Halliburton was thirty-nine, and either or both of us had the distinct possibility of never seeing another sunrise. I will remember that morning forever. The frost clinging to the grass and trees. The blue grey of the Atlantic Ocean beyond

the point and the bite of the wind off the water. The click of
the pistol case as it opened. The deathly cawing of two
ragged crows in a nearby pine. The quiet whispers of our
seconds as they tried to negotiate a last-minute truce. When
the word *fire* was given, Halliburton let go with a volley that
missed me clearly and hit a nearby tree, spraying chunks of
birchbark about. I took one look at young Halliburton, his
brow damp with perspiration, and deloped, firing into the
air. Honour had been served. I never intended to fire at him
and would not for ten thousand pounds. I wanted no blood
upon my hands."

Joe pauses for a second as though winded by the intense
emotions the retelling of that long ago event has stirred up.

"Afterward we shook hands and I returned home to a
lively breakfast with dearest Susie and our babes as they
bounced on my knees. Why, I ate three poached eggs, five
rashers of bacon, and four pieces of bread with the finest
jam I had ever tasted."

"Joe, you left out one piece of the story. After the s-s-
smoke had cleared from Halliburton's shot, you took delib-
erate aim at him so that he would realize he was at your
mercy, exclaimed 'Let the creature live,' and *then* fired your
shot into the air before walking away."

"Quite so, Ennis. You see, I knew I must strike fear into
young Halliburton and his set so they would think twice
about challenging me again, otherwise I should not be able
to walk down Hollis Street without being challenged by my
opponents."

Seeing the two men together is fascinating. Joe has the
gaze of a proud father as he listens to Ennis speak, while
Ennis gives the older man the respectful deference only
offered by a beloved protégé.

"And yet Joe still faced challenges afterward. Why within

six weeks Sir Rupert George, the provincial secretary, challenged Joe for comments he made in which he contrasted Sir Rupert's s-s-significant income with his modest work habits and even more modest capabilities."

"Nonetheless I was able to avoid Sir Rupert's challenge, with my honour intact, simply because I had recently met young Halliburton's request. Why, of the many things I have forgotten from my past, and believe me, there are many, I still recall what I told his second in declining his request: Having never had any personal quarrel with Sir Rupert, I should certainly not fire at him if I went out, and I have no great fancy for being shot at whenever public officers whose abilities I happen to contrast with their stipends, think fit to consider my political arguments and general illustrations to be insolent and offensive."

"The public laughed at Sir Rupert, and no one blamed Joe for turning his challenge aside. Quite fortunate that, as Sir Rupert was a good sh-sh-shot and would have at least winged Joe."

"It was an important lesson for my future in politics. By going through the duel with Halliburton early in my career, I had shown my courage and willingness to take up my sword and run into battle. It made future opponents wary and gained me a great deal of respect amongst the general public. A fine lesson for all politicians, Erin."

In the quiet after they leave I'm left to wonder which duels I've been avoiding. I have a strength wrapped in a weakness or a weakness cloaked by a strength—I'm the Queen of Conflict Avoidance but also a good mediator between warring sides. From peacemaking on the school playground to moderating workplace disputes, I've always been the calm voice of reason. Maybe I need to "take up my sword" and join the fray more often.

CHAPTER 22

"You should've told me, Margie. I'm glad you did it, still you should've said something. Dunc is a dick, everyone knows that, but he's dangerous. He has a lot of sway with the premier. Not knowing what you were up to could've put me in a tight spot, that's all."

"You're absolutely right. I'm sorry, Erin. My apologies."

She's never called me Erin before. She's always careful to call me "Minister," even though she's the same age as my mother. I'm sitting in her office, the walls full of photos and awards from a long, successful career. University convocation photos of her son and daughter rest on a console table along with an action shot of her son driving to the hoop when he played basketball for the Saint Mary's University Huskies.

"As you know, deputies serve at the discretion of cabinet, so we can be terminated at any time, virtually without cause. Sadly, it teaches us to be very careful. I don't know if you realize it, but Dunc's recently retired DM was actually let go because of him."

"I had no idea. They announced that she retired."

"Technically true. The Premier's Office gave her the option of retirement or non-renewal of her contract. Pam had a great career, she's a bright woman and a great deputy, so she didn't want to go out under a dark cloud. It's not just Pam either. Dunc is responsible for four of his department's top five people leaving, and he's only been there two years. All of them were good, experienced people. Dunc didn't like how they rolled or that they wouldn't bend the facts to fit his bizarre plans. He raked a couple of them over the coals at a training conference for junior staff. He described a few others as 'incompetent' to a key stakeholder at a meeting while they sat squirming in the same boardroom. Dunc doesn't understand that while he's the minister, he's not his staff's boss, the deputy minister is. Pam tried to protect her staff and it cost her. We had a couple of vacancies, and Tom and Jenna were good fits, so I hired them."

"You did the right thing. Next time let's make sure we have the discussion first, though."

"Fair enough, Erin."

"Now let's figure out how I'm going to pitch those programs to cabinet given that Dunc will be out to shoot them down, not only because they infringe on his main department's territory, but also because of your hirings."

"So you see, for $250,000, each of these new programs can do some targeted good, both in rural and urban Nova Scotia. The grants would range from $5,000 to $10,000 and could be spread across a number of districts if we have suitable applicants. We estimate community groups in thirty to forty districts across the province will be able to access one or other of the programs and host nutritionists or physical trainers."

Seventeen of my eighteen colleagues around the cabinet table look pleased. They seem to like the good they could accomplish at little cost. The opportunity to spread some money around their districts strikes a positive chord too. While the premier isn't smiling his big, warm smile, he isn't frowning either. I did the presentation without my DM in the room, which is unusual. We agreed that her presence might piss off Dunc.

"Do you have any concerns, Dunc?" the premier asks, in a move obviously orchestrated beforehand.

Dunc looks up from the iPhone he is constantly playing with as if he knows how to use the damn thing, which I doubt. I don't know how he can even get it to work with his huge hands and sausage-sized fingers.

My EA, Mackenzie Chisholm, warned me to be careful with Dunc. She's normally smiling and upbeat but turned deadly serious, almost fearful, when talking about him. She says he treats the caucus office staff like servants and never forgets any perceived lack of deference to him.

"Premier, I have a number of concerns. First about committing to spend half a million new dollars."

"Sorry to interrupt, Dunc, it's not new monies. We're going to fund them from my department's existing budget."

"It's still new programs, Erin, so politically it looks like you're spending new money. Once you've been in this game as long as I have, you'll realize that the folks down at Tim Hortons don't understand the difference. They already think we spend like drunken sailors, just not on the right things. Besides that, these two programs fall under the jurisdiction of my Community Development department. You can't have departments going willy-nilly into each other's fields and planting crops."

"Premier, if I might. I recognize that these programs are certainly on the borderline between the responsibilities of Dunc's department and mine, but we have the staff capacity and the money to make them happen. I'm sure Dunc and his people would've come up with something similar if they weren't busy with other government priorities. Unlike Dunc, who carries quite a load, I don't have responsibility for any of our government's major priorities. Why not give us approval to give it a go? If they don't succeed, it can be put down to an error in judgement by an inexperienced cabinet minister."

Nathalie, sitting across the table, gives me a discreet thumbs-up.

"Thanks, folks, we've heard enough on this and we've got a full agenda. I think it's pretty clear that cabinet wishes to approve these programs. Dunc raised some legitimate concerns though. Let's call them pilot programs for now, and we can re-evaluate them next year. Okay, moving on."

The premier unilaterally decides to approve the item as he often does, speaking for the room, unless opinions are clearly divided, and then he calls for a vote by show of hands. Nathalie and a few other people voice support and no one objects other than Dunc, so he rolls with it. As I gather up my papers at the end of the meeting, I see that Dunc has pushed his way through the throng of executive assistants, Premier's Office staff, and public servants that have swarmed into the room.

"We'll see how this turns out, Erin. We wouldn't want your first venture as a minister to be a big flop. After all,

you're our rising female star in Metro," he says with a sneer.
"By the way, make sure you tell your deputy she hired
herself a couple of real troublemakers. The PO won't be too
happy that you allowed it to happen, neither. You have yourself a nice day."

CHAPTER 23

Robbie and I have been going through the roughest patch in our ten-year marriage. Weeks without intimacy, without laughter. Long periods of barely civil conversation. Fights that strike like lightning. And silences. Long, painful, heartbreakingly lonely silences.

The jealousy injected into our relationship by my being in cabinet doubled yesterday when an old friend from Robbie's caucus office days came to town. He's now the chief of staff for a powerful federal cabinet minister. He and Robbie got together for dinner and drinks to trade old war stories. I stayed home with Zoey. God knows I owe Robbie one. This morning he's hungover and grouchy. Instead of thanking me for letting him go out with his buddy, I get the cold shoulder for most of the day. I can't take it any longer.

"So, what's up? You've been a bear all day," I say, after finally getting Zoey settled for the night.

"Nothing. I'm tired. I'm not used to going out on the town anymore."

I let the remark pass. He's on the couch with the TV

remote, switching from TSN to CNN to CBC Newsworld and back again. It's one of his more annoying habits.

"Shaun's just back from the summit in Davos. Before that he and the minister were in Berlin and London for conferences. Last month he was in Rio and the month before, Tokyo and Seoul."

"I guess when you're chief of staff for the Minister of Foreign Affairs travel goes with the gig. It's probably the upside and the downside of the job. Good thing he's an unattached, single guy. Actually, it's probably why he's an unattached, single guy. When Zoey's older we'll be able to do more travelling again."

"It's not only the travel or the big job, Erin, he's going to run in the next election. Shaun's moving back here to seek the nomination for West Nova, and he's got a pretty good shot at it. Christ, a year from now he could be an MP."

"Robbie, you could run too. It was your choice not to follow through on the nomination. I didn't stop you. You chose not to run."

"I chose not to get obliterated. After the *HFX Candid* story, I didn't have much of a chance of winning the nomination and even less of winning an election. That's a fact and now that you're in elected politics, you know I'm right."

I try not to engage, a new tactic. But no luck.

"It's not only that," Robbie continues, clearly on a roll. "One of the older lawyers called me into his office a few days ago and said the senior partners were concerned about how I was balancing my work time with my family life."

"What's wrong with that? He's telling you that they value work–life balance."

"Don't be naïve. No senior male partner tells a young, male lawyer to worry about his home life. What he's really saying is that all my leaving early to get Zoey before the daycare closes is getting noticed. Other junior lawyers are in the office until at least seven, maybe later. The partners see me leaving at four thirty and view it as a junior billing clients 2.5 hours less per day. That's more than twelve hours a week fewer billable hours. To them, I'm stealing money out of their pockets. They're not happy."

Robbie's jaw and cheek muscles are tightening, as they do when he's angry. My tell is blotches of crimson red skin on my face and neck that aren't attractive. I don't dare look in the mirror right now.

Law is a glorified pyramid scheme where the billable hours compiled by young junior lawyers help create the wealth that gets split up among the senior partners. Billable hours are a big deal, and by that standard Robbie's not measuring up. He's not saying this is all my fault, but he may as well. We both know that my schedule makes it tough for me to pick up Zoey.

"And while I'm not making the grade at the office, I come home and there's only me and Zoey. You're back late, or you have to go out for evening events, or you collapse on the couch and fall asleep. It's like you're not here for me anymore. What's worse is you're not here for Zoey either."

He cuts me with scalpel-like precision only a spouse can inflict, going right for my weak spot. I feel guilty as hell about my time away from Robbie and Zoey. Every new word or goofy antic of hers that I miss piles on the guilt.

"That's totally unfair. You know damn well that before I was in cabinet the shoe was on the other foot. When you started with MacKay and Macdonald there were lots of times when you barely got home in time to kiss Zoey good night. I watched a lot of Netflix, sitting alone on this couch waiting for you."

I wound too. I know that because of Robbie's workaholic

father, he is very conscientious about wanting to do better on the father–husband front. His mom taught him to ride a bike and throw a baseball and was the parent who attended all the school events. His dad was always at the office or out shaking hands.

I storm out of the living room and go upstairs to bed, rigid with anger and unspoken words. Even after Robbie comes to bed, I toss and turn, my body on high alert. Between the pressures of cabinet and walking on eggshells at home, I'm exhausted.

CHAPTER 24

"No doubt, Erin, the smallness of politics can be trying, especially when one gets to the senior levels as you now find yourself, a member of cabinet and a growing leader in your party."

"Oh, I'd hardly call myself a leader in the party."

"On the contrary, your political colleagues speak very highly of your rising status. They are greatly impressed with your efforts, both yours and those of your friend Miss Amirault."

"I'm so tired of our government not having any ambition about what we want to achieve. Our only goal is to grasp tightly to power and never let it go. It makes me doubt my decision to go into politics."

"Indeed, politics can be like that at times. Remember the words of the immortal Shakespeare: 'Our doubts are traitors, and make us lose the good we oft might win, by fearing to attempt.' Granted, it is much more exciting, more enervating when one has a substantial goal on the horizon that one is striving to reach, be it building a railway, growing the commerce of our country, or bringing responsible government to Nova Scotia."

"Now those are goals. That's direction."

"Yes, one could argue that attaining responsible government was one of the crowning achievements of my political career, perhaps my most enduring victory for our beloved Nova Scotia. And one of the most difficult too. It took myself and my fellow Reformers, Herbert Huntington, James Boyle Uniacke, and Laurence O'Connor Doyle, ten long, arduous years to reach that goal, but by God we did it."

"Joe, I'm not entirely sure I understand how responsible government differs from what Nova Scotia had before."

"It is like chalk and cheese. What we had before gave Nova Scotians virtually no say in the running of their affairs or the spending of monies raised through taxation. An appointed governor arrived from England and governed with the help of an appointed Executive Council of twelve men, chosen from the wealthy class of businessmen and lawyers, that held all legislative and executive power. They administered the government, passed legislation, made the regulations, and appointed men to various paid government positions. They held the purse strings."

I'm still confused. "But we had an elected legislature for nearly one hundred years before we achieved responsible government."

"Yes, nonetheless its powers were few and its desires could be thwarted at every turn by the governor and his council. None of the council members were elected by the people, and as a class they disdained democratic politics. These council positions stayed within a web of interconnected families, primarily from Halifax and Church of England members, who in turn assured that paid government positions stayed within the web too. Council positions and government posts passed from father to son. No man could gain entry into this inner circle based solely on his abilities or achievements."

A troubling question comes to mind. How different is that Executive Council from today's unelected Premier's Office staff who, with the premier, run our government? A chuckle from Joe breaks this disturbing train of thought.

"The council of twelve knew nothing about most of the country they governed. Tom Haliburton used to say that two-thirds of them had never been beyond the Sackville River Bridge. And yet these fellows seemed unable to be evicted from this inner circle through incompetence. And so it remained, generation after generation, as they filled their pockets with government emoluments paid for by the good people of Nova Scotia."

"God, it was like the Mafia or organized crime, with the governor as the don. I had no idea the council was so all controlling."

"This was why Reformers such as myself and Doyle ran for office, I for the first time in 1836 in Halifax County. I was elected by a one-thousand-vote majority under the banner of 'Joe Howe, our Patriot and Reformer.' Of course, elections in those days were a far cry from the genteel tea parties you hold today."

"What do you mean?"

"During my first years in politics, provincial elections did not happen simultaneously in every district on the same day. Instead, elections involved the sheriff of each county moving from community to community in order to record each freeholder's vote. The sheriff erected a hustings, no more than a raised platform, usually outside the courthouse, and freeholders came forward and publicly announced their votes, which the sheriff carefully recorded in a ledger. In a large county like Annapolis, the hustings might be erected in four or five different communities. It could take days, even weeks to complete the entire provincial election."

"I don't understand the part about freeholders voting. What's a freeholder?"

"Why, it is a man of property. Someone who owns a home and land. One had to be a freeholder in order to be eligible to vote. Of course, the freeholder provision excluded eight in every ten men in Halifax from voting. In those days we called it the 'manly' act of voting, and for good reason. A freeholder had to make his way up to the hustings to announce his vote by forging a passageway through the heaving crowd. If the other side's supporters were nearby, it was like running a gauntlet, with many a kick to the shins and elbow to the stomach or face on the way to exercise your democratic right. All sides hosted open houses during elections, which added to the mayhem, as one's political supporters were plied with free drink, food, and tobacco to boost their courage before heading to the hustings."

"It sounds chaotic, undemocratic, and exceptionally male."

"Touché, Erin. Now, back to 1836 and our days as newly elected Reformers. When the Legislature reconvened after the election, we set to work. First, Doyle moved a resolution in the House to open wide the doors of the Executive Council so that our fellow Nova Scotians could see it in sordid and self-serving action. At that point it met behind closed doors, like Henry VII's secretive Star Chamber. My maiden speech in the House was on this very topic, with all the great Tory guns waiting in the wings to shoot me down."

Joe pauses for a moment, looking up at the ceiling of the

Uniacke Room as he tries to retrieve from memory a moment in his long career.

"If I recall, I said something along the lines of us asking for 'nothing but justice and responsibility, sanctioned by the spirit and forms of the British Constitution...etcetera, etcetera...and give to my country the blessed privilege of her constitution and her laws...let us be contented with nothing less.' Something of that sort. The House passed Doyle's resolution unanimously, even though we Reformers did not control the numbers, for the resolution's reasonableness was not in dispute. And yet, the Executive Council treated the resolution like one does an opponent's shuttlecock in a game of badminton and promptly returned it. They responded haughtily that His Majesty's Council denied the right of the House to comment upon its modes and procedure. They added further that whether their deliberations were open or secret was only of their concern, and theirs alone."

Once again, I could pinch myself. What Nova Scotia historian or political junkie wouldn't kill to be in my seat, having Joe Howe explain the battle for responsible government?

"And so the game of cat and mouse began, and at the beginning we were the mouse. Yet, we Reformers knew what we wanted to achieve. We wanted the men who held office and who carried on the business of Nova Scotia to be appointed by an executive that had the confidence of a majority of the members of the House, as was the case in our mother country."

In the midst of Joe's explanation of a turning point in Nova Scotia history a ridiculous question pops into my head: Did Robbie remember to put the chicken wings in the slow cooker this morning like I told him to?

"I proposed a series of resolutions decrying the current unrepresentative form of government and its subsequent abuses and urging approval to write an address to His Majesty to enunciate our desire for responsible government. In the resolutions I contrasted what existed in England and the genius of its institutions, whose complete responsibility is to the people, with the situation in Nova Scotia. Here, the people and its elected representatives were powerless, exercising little influence and no effectual control on the Executive Council. Whereas in England, the people by one vote of their representatives could change the government and alter any course of policy injurious to their interests."

As Joe talks, hundreds of former politicians look down on us from the room's walls, which are covered by group photos of members of various legislative sittings, all beneficiaries of Joe's legacy. For a moment the faces of these long dead politicians turn toward us from their framed homes as though our conversation has piqued their interest.

"In support of my resolutions, I delivered an eight-hour speech to the House and the crowded public gallery. The best of the Tory members spoke against me, and while they did not shoot down my resolutions, they left some with holes through them like Swiss cheeses."

Passion grows in Joe's voice as twitches of his bushy eyebrows accentuate every key point.

"The argument of the Tories ran thus: responsible government was not only irrelevant, but incompatible in practice with imperial authority and would inevitably lead to conflict between ourselves and Mother England and ultimately lead to Republicanism. I responded that the idea of Republicanism and independence, of severance from the mother country, never crossed my mind. I was and am a loyal British subject. I merely wanted what every Briton took for granted. My resolutions passed, but some were amended. Yet the substance of them remained and were wrapped up in an address sent to His Majesty. And so the battle raged between Reformers and the Tories for much of a decade."

I have to admit that the back and forth between Joe, the British Colonial Office, and the various governors and lords on the quest for responsible government is as confusing as studying the road to repatriation of the Canadian Constitution in 1982.

"At the same time more radical Reformers in the Canadas, William Lyon Mackenzie in Upper Canada, and Louis-Joseph Papineau in Lower Canada, pushed for American-style reforms. We temperately argued for a British model with an organized party system whose leaders held seats in the Legislature and answered directly to it. The more aggressive, and sometimes violent, actions of the Canadian Reformers were continuously thrown in the face of we Nova Scotia Reformers and did not assist our cause, and more than likely hampered it."

I'm about to ask Joe a question when the heavy door of the Uniacke Room swings open. I turn from the table to see George, one of the Legislature's security guards, entering and about to turn off the light.

"My apologies, Ms. Curran, I didn't realize you were in here. I just came on shift and no one mentioned that any of the meeting rooms were still in use. Busy, eh?"

"Catching up on some paperwork and decided to watch a YouTube clip on my laptop before I pack up."

My computer is open in front of me, and I have notes spread on the table. I've learned as best I can to hide my conversations with Joe, but it's getting harder. I only add the bit about watching YouTube in case George heard voices, although the door is so thick, it's unlikely.

George begins to cough before clearing his throat a couple of times.

"Sorry, I have a funny taste in my mouth. Sort of metallic. Must be something I ate. Don't you work too late. It can get right eerie around here late at night with some peculiar sounds. Have a nice evening." With that he leaves, closing the door behind him.

"Seems like a pleasant chap. I must tell you an aside. During those challenging times, Susie and I lived in accommodations on Spring Garden Road. Our neighbour was Joseph Keefler, a kindly old fellow who was sexton of St. Paul's Church, responsible for the church graveyard and such. In those days I was much in demand and called upon at all hours, day and night. Unfortunately, my friends and colleagues sometimes mistook Keefler's home for my own. These mistaken knocks on his door began to wear on the poor man. One night, Will Annand knocked and aroused the exhausted fellow's furor when he answered the door. 'Is Mr. Howe in?' Will asked. Keefler responded, 'No, he is not. He don't live here. He is killing the Tories. Joe Howe slays the Tories, and Joe Keefler buries them. I'm Joe Keefler, blast you. Go to the next house, or to pot if you like.'"

I try to contain my laughter, to not bring George running. Joe kills me. He's such a great storyteller.

"Where was I? Oh yes, leading up to the election in 1847, the first with simultaneous polling in every district in the province. It was a hectic campaign in which I spoke sixty times in ninety days, including near here at the Halifax public market adjacent to the ferry landing. I was cheered by shipbuilders in Hants, fishermen in Sambro, and the Scots of Cape Breton. I even addressed a gathering of nearly one thousand German settlers in Lunenburg, who had always supported the Tories. I had expected them to break my head, and instead they carried me off in triumph and elected our candidates."

"It must have been exciting, but absolutely exhausting."

"Quite so, yet well worth the toil and tumult. That election gave Reformers—we now called ourselves Liberals or Reformers interchangeably—a large majority in every county in Nova Scotia. We had stormed the hill and crested the summit. The election not only swept the Tories from power and from all government offices, it also assured that we had responsible government. Henceforth, every elected government must resign if it no longer has the support of the majority in the House. At last, we had the full rights of British subjects. It was a glorious time. After a decade we had at last achieved our objective. James Boyle Uniacke became premier, and I was appointed provincial secretary. So while Mackenzie led a failed armed rebellion in Upper Canada in 1837 to try and gain responsible government, we achieved our goal in Nova Scotia without one blow struck or pane of glass broken."

Joe pauses as though struck by some thought, taking the time to turn it over in his mind.

"We had an unparalleled victory, and I was all of forty-three years old. I spent another twenty-five years in active politics, and yet 1848 may well have been the height of my political career."

These last words seem to deflate him. His animated eyes grow dim, and he drops his leonine head. The vigour drains out of his body as if this thought is a revelation to him. Hours later as I fall asleep, I can't forget the sadness that wrapped about him.

CHAPTER 25

Why me? I've talked to Joe a dozen times over the past few months and I still can't figure out why, out of thousands of people who've walked the halls of Province House over 150 years, he has only connected with me.

Why not one of the dozens of premiers who have served since his passing? Surely a chat with Liberal icon Angus L. Macdonald or Tory idol Robert Stanfield would've been more interesting to Joe than talking to a neophyte politician like me. Wouldn't swapping political tales with John Buchanan have been a lot more fun than listening to a young cabinet minister whine?

Ennis hinted once that Joe was initially drawn to me because I apparently have the same nose and eyes as Joe's wife, Susan Ann.

"Even more than that, Erin, it is your combination of fiery spirit and calm resolve that he finds so fetching and familiar. Beneath Susan Ann's serene demeanour beat a steady and brave heart that did not flinch in the face of peril.

He sees that in you. Joe is drawn to that quality as a moth to a flame."

Sometimes I wonder what Joe is trying to teach me. Maybe he's hoping to pass on a shortcut as I make my way through the maze of Nova Scotia politics or is counselling me on what I need in order to grow as a person. He loved teaching his apprentices at the *Novascotian*. Maybe to him I'm like one of those raw trainees, only in a different trade with much to learn.

Our conversations have a Socratic air to them. Me asking questions about his life and accomplishments that sometimes offer perspective on my problems. Joe leading those conversations in ways that often leave me with other, deeper questions. Among those is what I want to achieve while I'm in office and whether I even want to continue in political life with all its challenges.

Maybe it's best not to question the why of Joe's connection to me and instead accept the wonder of it. To soak up all the knowledge he offers and find a way to make it relevant to me and my times.

CHAPTER 26

I've been complaining to Robbie for weeks about some of the stuff that cabinet has approved for funding lately. I say lately, but for all I know it was happening before I was appointed too. Time and time again, cabinet allows rural municipalities to skip paying their share of funding for infrastructure or programs that involve joint, provincial–municipal funding. Instead, the province pays its share and most or all of the rural municipality's share too.

There's no real pattern to it, although places represented by our members are most likely to benefit. Sometimes though it's Opposition districts that our party sees as potential pickups in the next election. Other times it's simply cabinet's belief that without waiving the municipal portion of funding, the project won't happen and we want it to happen.

You could charitably describe it as the provincial government lending a helping hand to communities in need. Fair enough. Still, I suspect that Halifax taxpayers would riot in the streets if they realized they shoulder this largesse because Halifax almost always pays its portion. It rarely gets a break. So, Halifax taxpayers pay their municipal share for projects inside Halifax and sometimes, via provincial taxes, double pay for projects outside Halifax.

What's worse is this money often goes to regions that turn their backs on municipal amalgamation, which would create larger, more efficient municipal units that might pull their weight financially. Yet, for fear of a backlash, our government never pressures inefficient, smaller municipalities to amalgamate. In a way, we reward them for refusing necessary municipal reform.

"It's the nature of politics, especially here, but really anywhere in Canada," Robbie says, trying to talk me out of my rant. "Government has to show it's on top of things and can solve problems, even if it's some other level of government's fault. Sometimes showing progress comes at a cost."

"Fair enough, so long as everyone in the province knows what's going on, that taxpayers in Halifax and other thriving parts of Nova Scotia are carrying the weight for the rest. But do they, Robbie? I don't think so."

Sometimes I think Nova Scotia only has a handful of fully functioning municipalities. The rest are municipalities in name only. I'll have to take this up with Joe tonight. We have late-night debate on some pressing issue, like is Nova Scotia doing enough to combat light pollution? Or should nurses be issued special emergency responder licence plates? Late debate is a cynical political platform for parties to show the public how much they care about one "critical" issue or another, which the parties probably don't know a lot about yet want to be seen to support.

"Yes, Erin, I understand your concern and it has been ever thus, but one must appreciate the causes. Haligonians forget their many blessings are not shared throughout our land. Since the beginning we have benefited from hosting the British Navy and later the Canadian Navy and all the commerce that brings. Add to that the benefit of being the capital of our province and the various clerks, inspectors, and such in its employ, most of whom are situated in Halifax. Our fair city is also the seat of governance for the various religious denominations and home to many fine universities with lecturers and such. Our rural countrymen have none of those advantages, or few of them, and rural Nova Scotia has limited financial wherewithal. As Tom Haliburton's famous character Sam Slick liked to say: 'You can't get blood from a stone.'"

We are talking in the Legislative Library, though I am growing wary about this. My spider senses are tingling. I have the feeling that my movements around here are being tracked. I'm becoming as paranoid as the rest of my colleagues in this fishbowl. When the Legislature is in session, politicians of various stripes, EAs, staff, civil servants, and reporters mill about a breath away from each other for months in this house of whispers.

"With Halifax's financial advantages have come cultural ones—stage plays, orchestras, libraries, newspapers. No, we have a wise gardener's responsibility to help grow and nurture our rural communities until they blossom as Halifax has done. And if that requires a good watering of coins from the provincial coffers from time to time, so be it."

"I see your argument, Joe, and agree with parts of it. Fair enough. But don't we have a responsibility as politicians to be transparent about our actions? To ensure Halifax taxpayers know they are paying more than their fair share? If our reason is valid, shouldn't we make it public?"

"I concede you the point. You are a fine debater. I think a good politician could certainly make the argument for greater largesse for our rural folk, for truly they are the lifeblood of this great province. I am a Haligonian, born and bred, from my earliest days as a boy swimming in the North-west Arm to my last feeble ones in my sick bed at Government House. Other than a brief sojourn in Ottawa, I spent my life here. Nonetheless, my rambles, from the mountains of Cape Breton to the fecund fields of the Annapolis Valley, taught me that the spirit of Nova Scotia is in our rural parts. My two years living on Will Annand's farm in Upper Musquodoboit were the final master class on the subject."

"You lived in Upper Musquodoboit? When was that?"

"From 1845 until 1847. You see, by the spring of '45 I was exhausted from all the effort required to push for reform. I was forty years old and needed a respite from my travails. Will Annand and his brother, James, were kind enough to host dear Susie and me and our growing brood in a cottage on their farm. It was a delightful time in my life. Absolutely splendid. To spend the day working with one's back and hands in the fields in the fine country air did me a world of good."

"Joe Howe the farmer. I find that hard to imagine."

"It was wonderful for Susie and me. We could peacefully sit down after dinner and not be constantly disrupted, day and night, by political allies seeking my advice as we had been in the city. We had fine company with the Annands and their neighbours in that valley, some of the best folk I ever met. This may surprise you, but were it not for the incoming tide of support for responsible government, I might have retired to the countryside and that rustic way of life. Yet, destiny was calling and something always drove me to answer its call."

"Look, there's no question that rural Nova Scotia helps define this place, but it still needs to pay its way. The Scots who fled the Highland Clearances, Acadians who returned after the Grand Derangement, the demobbed English soldiers, American planters, Black Loyalists, German settlers, they all moved to rural Nova Scotia for a reason: because they thought they could support their families there. They didn't settle there for the wonderful view and a slower pace of life. If these rural places can no longer sustain themselves economically, should we as a Government continue to support or subsidize them? They may have two hundred years or more of their people buried in the local cemetery, but would their forefathers have stayed if they couldn't make a living? If they couldn't support themselves? That's the question."

"And it is a troubling one, Erin. I might only add that aside from money and commerce and the provincial coffers, there are the people to consider too. People like you and me see the larger outside world and are excited by the novel experiences it has to offer, and we embrace it. We have skills that enable us to make our way in the bigger world. Why, I myself could have been the editor of the *New York Albion* newspaper and moved to that great metropolis had I accepted William Morrell's generous offer."

"Anyone can leave Nova Scotia to take advantage of opportunities in the greater world."

"Not entirely true, Erin. There are those of our countrymen without skills to go out in the larger world and survive. More crucially, they have a desperate attachment to our homeland. It anchors and defines them. The St. Mary's River flows in their blood, Blomidon is their rock and comfort, the colourful splendour of Cape Breton in the fall is their sustenance. They are at sea without these touch-stones. Are they to be thrown to the wolves? You are young and full of the vigour demanded to address such pressing questions. Thank goodness for that, and I leave you to it. Good evening, Erin."

CHAPTER 27

"And so I ask the Minister of Education how the elementary school in Upper Middlewood went from being absent from her department's top-ten priority list for capital projects this year to yesterday's announcement of a ten-million-dollar renovation for a school with a declining student population?"

Opposition leader Danny Gillis has that smug look he gets when he thinks he's connected with a winning punch—and he has. We approved this last-minute addition to Education's annual capital list a couple of weeks ago. It's in Janet Zwicker's district, and there's no way in the world it would've received funding otherwise.

"My officials regularly adjust our capital projects list based on emerging maintenance challenges at our schools," Education Minister Pauline Salah responds to the first interesting question of today's Question Period. "Issues were brought to our attention that we felt demanded a prompt response to ensure the security and well-being of that school's students and teachers, and our government delivered."

The House is quieting as members grow interested in this exchange—or as quiet as fifty-one people can be who are shuffling papers, whispering to neighbours, asking the pages to run errands, or moving around in their chairs.

"I'm curious to know whether the minister can document what those maintenance concerns are, but I'll leave that for now," Gillis says, circling in for the kill. "What I would really like you to explain, Minister, is why this particular elementary school with its declining student population also required a new gymnasium built to the larger dimensions of a junior high school?"

"My staff and local municipal officials felt it was an opportunity to address the need in the local community for flexible space for after-school use."

"That's a very interesting answer, Minister," Gillis says, as the Opposition MLAs groan, laugh, and catcall the minister and Government MLAs across the floor with taunts from the playground.

"Which leads to my final question. Is the municipality or the local community providing funding for the additional space that's beyond the normal requirements for an elementary school gym? Are they funding this additional space as required under the regulations for the minister's own department, or is the provincial government?"

Gillis sits down like he raked in the pot at a high-stakes poker game in Vegas and is ready to head out on the town to party. In a few minutes he'll be scrummed by the Legislature reporters, and he'll double down on his bet.

"As I already told the Official Opposition leader, my officials and municipal officials are working together to address a larger need in the community," Pauline says, as the members on our side of the House sag and those across the aisle flush with victory.

She resorts to the non-answer answer. Nathalie and I argued against this project in cabinet. Everyone in the room knew it was trouble, but Janet wanted to deliver the goods to her district, and given she's a fierce ally of the premier, he backed her.

If the Opposition handles this right, it could be a multi-day story, the kind that sticks. The public can miss a one-day media story, no matter how big it is. They have demanding jobs, kids to feed and cart to hockey practice, and evening Netflix binges to satisfy. But anyone with a phone, TV, or car radio eventually comes across a multi-day story.

Given this is the second school controversy in less than two years in Janet's Bridgewater district, it's going to be a multi-day story. Before I won my by-election, Janet pulled the same trick and managed to get a new Bridgewater elementary school announced, leapfrogging other projects and landing on the capital priorities list from out of nowhere. That school is under construction.

OUR GOVERNMENT HAS BEEN PUMMELLED all week on the Upper Middlewood school renovation. The Opposition has played it well, with a different focus every day. First it was the school jumping the queue to be announced for renovations over more worthy and desperate priorities. Then it was the fact that government is paying the local municipality's share of additional funding required for the larger gymnasium. Finally, the angle was that rural schools with similarly declining student populations have been forced to close.

Three days of stories, which robbed Nathalie's announcement of the big economic development strategy of any positive play it might have had. It's a great piece of work that's well researched and thought out and offers some hope. Of course, the first questions the premier took from the media after he and Nathalie announced the strategy were about Upper Middlewood.

The premier is wearing this one, along with the education minister and of course Janet, because the media and public know that Upper Middlewood wouldn't have happened without her influence. LeBlanc is furious this is getting pinned on the premier. The announcement of the economic strategy got pushed back a day because of the school controversy in an unsuccessful effort not to rain on Nathalie's parade. Changing the date for Nathalie's announcement pushed back the public launch of my department's two new programs by a day too.

Despite that, both Nathalie and I got some positive press, at least from the *Chronicle*'s political columnist, Pam Carvery. After spending two-thirds of her latest column ripping the premier for a growing list of old-fashioned patronage, favouritism, and mismanagement, she gave Nathalie's announcement a shout-out. Nathalie's complex and future-looking approach got all of two small paragraphs of mention describing it as "intriguing" and "far-sighted." My department's two new programs got one long sentence ending with "which shows, as this columnist has said before, what can be accomplished with a limited and focused amount of government funding."

Then there are the few sentences at the end of the column that, while flattering, are going to cause us both trouble with our cabinet colleagues: "The careful, measured, and winning approach of these two new ministers stands in sharp contrast to the controversy-prone deadwood in the premier's cabinet that he needs to shed if he wants Nova Scotians to give him a third mandate."

"That Opposition-lovin' bitch knows full well that when Gillis's party was in Government their favourite projects jumped the government queues for approval all the time," LeBlanc fumed the other day after a caucus meeting.

Of course, the Opposition was last in power seven years ago, a lifetime ago to the public, but only the other day to partisans like LeBlanc who remember every slight against their party and every victory like most of us remember our family's birthdays and anniversaries. LeBlanc ignores the fact that if we'd followed the Education Department's policies, Upper Middlewood would never have been approved and we wouldn't be in hot water. We screwed up and are paying the price.

"If you want to dance, you have to pay the fiddler," Dad used to say about poor decisions when I was nursing a hangover in my university days.

In the world of politics, our members can never admit that our side screwed up. If we are under attack, we are always right and our opponents—the opposition parties, the media, and the public—are always wrong; they don't understand the issue or are simply naïve. There's not much owning up to mistakes, and like anyone dealing with complex issues, we make our fair share.

The Upper Middlewood controversy has caucus members grumbling again. I ran into Doug the other day, and he said a number of our members feel that the premier is far too loyal to the old guard. There's even whispers that if the premier doesn't dump them soon, maybe he's not the right guy to lead us into the next election.

"Doug, be very careful who you say that to. If LeBlanc or anyone heard that you said that, there'd be hell to pay."

"What are they going to do to me? Leave me to rot on the backbenches? Oh, wait, that's what I'm already doing. All

I'm saying is you better start thinking about who you would back if it comes to that. Some people say that Nathalie is the right person. And you know that's true."

"We could sure use someone who thinks like you in cabinet, Doug. Look after yourself."

Later, I made a point of running into Nathalie.

"Shit. I don't need paranoid people like Dunc or LeBlanc thinking that I'm trying to knife the premier, or I won't get any more initiatives through cabinet. They'll cut me off at the knees."

"I thought you'd want to know. Be careful, Nathalie. Right now, the Premier's Office thinks that anyone else's success reflects poorly on the premier. Lie low. Maybe you should put some of your initiatives on the backburner."

"I understand what you're saying and appreciate the heads-up, but I really believe the things we're working on have merit. God knows we can't wait to turn our economy around."

"Then make certain the premier gets some credit and most of the limelight the next time you announce something. And Doug's right, some day you would look good sitting at the front of the cabinet table. The first Acadian and the first female premier ever."

"For God's sake, don't ever say that to anyone. Not even Robbie. Promise?"

CHAPTER 28

"So you want to talk about my Confederation battles? I hope you have a large portion of time on your hands, Erin, for it is not a story easily told, nor a pretty one."

We are in the Veterans Room shortly after debate on the budget estimates wrapped up in the House. It's nearly seven p.m. and I have some time because I thought we'd be sitting longer—I told Robbie not to expect me before nine. Shadows gather in the corners of the room in the late spring evening. In daytime, when sunlight shines on the cream-coloured walls, this is one of the happiest rooms I know, but at night it's sombre, perhaps a fitting location to talk to Joe about Confederation, the most controversial period of his lengthy political career.

Joe has long been attacked for leading the charge against Nova Scotia joining Confederation. He opposed it with all of his powers of persuasion, taking on the formidable Dr. Charles Tupper, Nova Scotia's premier at the time and Confederation's strongest local supporter. The two were fierce political foes. Dubbed "the Fighting Doctor," which would make a good Twitter handle, Tupper gave Joe his first electoral defeat in 1855 in Cumberland County where Tupper lived and practised medicine. The result threw Joe out of provincial political office for the first time in nearly twenty years.

Why Joe opposed Confederation has long been debated. Some historians think his ego and personal dislike of Tupper were behind it. Others believe he opposed Confederation because he hadn't been in Charlottetown at the beginning of its conception and as a result had no ownership of the plan.

"I will not play second fiddle to that damn'd Tupper," Joe is famously believed to have said.

Despite strong anti-Confederation feelings in Nova Scotia, Tupper and his allies in the Canadas and in the British Colonial Office managed to achieve Confederation in 1867. Yet, in the Nova Scotia provincial election of September 1867, thirty-six of thirty-eight seats were taken by the Anti-Confederation Party. And in the first federal election after Confederation, Joe barnstormed across Nova Scotia with his Anti-Confederate allies, leading them to victory in eighteen of nineteen federal seats, including Howe's new seat in Hants County. The only pro-Confederate MP elected was Tupper in Cumberland. The Anti-Confederate goal was to unmake the Confederation cake, which had already been baked and served.

Fate, pride, or Nova Scotia patriotism eventually led Joe to switch sides and enter Sir John A. Macdonald's first Canadian cabinet, despite being elected to the House of Commons as the leader of the Anti-Confederates. It was a flip-flop that dogged Joe for the rest of his days, making enemies of long-time friends and raising doubts about his motivations.

"My battle against Confederation, and my eventually being overcome by it, is a long and sad tale. Confederation was like a riptide that dragged me back into politics. Swimming against it drained me and came at immeasurable personal cost."

Joe is talking quietly, his eyes locked on the fireplace's white mantlepiece and not on me in his normally friendly way. He's in this room, but the memories have thrust him back more than 150 years to the turbulent streets, meeting rooms, and barns of Nova Scotia in the mid-1860s in the midst of a political firestorm.

"It all began rather oddly when Dr. Tupper reached out in 1864 and asked me to be in the Nova Scotia delegation to a conference on the potential union of the Maritime provinces to be held in Charlottetown. This idea had been talked about, on and off, for many years. You must remember, Erin, that the Charlottetown Conference that everyone now speaks of as the beginning of Canada was not called to propose anything of the sort but rather to discuss Maritime union. Representatives from Upper and Lower Canada were not initially invited and sought permission to attend."

"I had no idea. The way we're taught history is that all the founding fathers went to Charlottetown with the goal of building a new country, and that was Canada."

"Far from it. Regardless, I declined Dr. Tupper's invitation as I was serving as Imperial Fisheries Commissioner and my participation in such a political discussion would have been inappropriate. Added to that, I was scheduled to be on the water off Prince Edward Island and Newfoundland aboard the HMS *Lily* for an inspection. The talks at the so-called Charlottetown Conference developed into a full-blown discussion of Confederation, no doubt as the Canadians and the British Colonial Office had hoped. It seems the British government saw a union of their North American colonies as a way of reducing expenses and commitments, particularly military ones. And where was I in the midst of all this intrigue? Seasick off the coast of Labrador. The Charlottetown Conference led to a further meeting in October 1864 in Quebec City, and the rest, as they say, is history."

"Joe, we have a saying that it's not over until it's over. It seems that you didn't accept that Confederation was inevitable, before or after Confederation."

"I did not, and certainly many Nova Scotians felt the same. By the beginning of the winter of '64–'65 I was more convinced than ever that Confederation would be a grievously mistaken path for Nova Scotia to take. It was too radical and an affront to our British heritage."

"It's hard for Nova Scotians today to understand why you opposed Confederation. We're proud Canadians. Canada is a great country. We have a good economy, free health care, a great post-secondary education system. We're a multicultural nation—it's part of our identity and it seems to work for us. Canada's safe and peaceful and wildly beautiful with liveable big cities. It's not perfect, especially for Indigenous Peoples and Canadians of colour, and still has challenges for women as well as the gay, lesbian, and transgendered communities, but even so it's better than most countries. So why were you so concerned about joining together to form a new country?"

"A number of points worried me. Amongst the greatest was Nova Scotia being swamped by all those damnable Canadians," Joe says, rising to his feet as he hooks his left hand in the lapel of his frock coat, feet firmly apart as if to rise to the attack.

"We were about to throw our lot in with more than three

and a half million others and counted only 350,000 souls in our homeland. I feared that a system built on representation by population would put our small numbers in a position of weakness when it came to political appointments, control of the post office, taxation, as well as the regulation of shipping, navigation, and fisheries that were our lifeblood."

"Your fears about Nova Scotia's power within Canada being overwhelmed by the sheer population of Ontario and Quebec and the political clout that gives them turned out to be valid."

"Indeed so. Confederation was also in direct opposition to a far more ambitious plan I had put forward to reinvigorate the British Empire through a reorganization that would enable the fine colonial politicians I had met over the years to contribute their inestimable capabilities on behalf of their Queen. I felt our colony needed to evolve to a more equitable relationship within the Empire that would allow us to draw even closer to the bosom of Britain. I feared Confederation would tear us from the breast of the Empire and bring us closer to the Canadians and perhaps even our wayward American cousins."

"So when did The Botheration Scheme letters start appearing? They're quite the letters."

A smile briefly cracks the serious face Joe has worn throughout our discussion of Confederation.

"The first appeared on the eleventh of January, 1865, in the *Morning Chronicle* while I was concluding my term as Imperial Fisheries Commissioner. It was soon followed by eleven other letters. They were anonymous, nonetheless my unique style of writing and particular use of language quickly alerted readers to their authorship."

"If those letters are any indication, you'd be the perfect fit on the creative team of any marketing firm today. For an

Anti-Confederate to describe Confederation as The Bother-ation Scheme was brilliant."

"Thank you. I quite liked it myself. It made light of a serious matter in a way I felt underscored the absurdity of what was being proposed. My goal was to stress to the dear readers of the *Morning Chronicle* that it would be difficult, and more likely impossible, to devise a federation with the Canadas that would be properly balanced. I also empha-sized to our countrymen the dangers of handing the management of Nova Scotia affairs over to the Canadians. One could not trust them. They were eccentric, at times even rebellious, and they were led by political tricksters."

"I also liked your line about Sampson and Delilah in one of the letters. Something like 'was Sampson stronger when Delilah got him confederated, bound him up, and cut off his hair?'"

"Another popular quip I used a hundred times on speaking platforms across our country, from the steps of the Queens County Courthouse to the Covenanter Church in Grand Pré, was an attack on the financial terms of the initial deal to provide Nova Scotia with eighty cents per head in federal subsidies for entering into Confederation. We were sold for the price of a sheepskin, I said over and over to huge applause. My objections to the scheme grew stronger and more profound when it became clear that Dr. Tupper had no intention whatsoever to put Confederation, the most critical political decision of our generation, before the people of Nova Scotia in an election to deter-mine its fate. His chicanery denied Nova Scotians the political freedom we had worked so hard to achieve in 1848."

Joe has grown stone-faced again as he talks about Confederation and Dr. Tupper. I don't know whether it's the subject or talk of the Cumberland doctor or both that have closed his normally open face.

"Damn his eyes, that side-whiskered bulldog used every political tool at his disposal—patronage, senatorships, and whatnot—to ensure his resolution in the Legislature supporting Confederation successfully crossed the finish line. This may surprise someone of your time, but July 1, 1867, was greeted in many parts of Nova Scotia with the sombreness that follows the passing of an old friend. Few pro-Canadian flags flew. Some people flew black flags or Union Jacks at half-mast. Some newspapers printed funereal black borders around their front pages with headlines that decried the state of affairs. An editorial in New Glasgow's *Eastern Chronicle* went so far as to describe the newborn Dominion of Canada as an 'illegitimate child.'"

"From what I've read it's not unlike how many Newfoundlanders greeted their entry into Canada in 1949, like a death in the family. So, Joe, you ended up in Ottawa as a federal MP for a country you didn't believe should exist. What happened?"

"I led a delegation of my fellow Anti-Confederates to London to lobby British politicians and the Colonial Office to repeal the British North America Act, the legislation that enabled Confederation. Frankly, I had grave doubts about our chance of success. It seemed a doomed adventure, although fortunately I was able to take Susan Ann and Ennis with me."

"In gambling casinos they would describe it as 'the fix being in,' meaning the Colonial Office held all the cards so that you had no chance of winning."

"I am not a great man for cards or gambling—I did more than enough gambling in my business and political affairs —yet that is a very apt description of our chances of success.

Naturally, we ran into that damnable Tupper while in London. He took me aside and poured honeyed words in my ears for two solid hours. 'You are here to obtain a repeal of the Union,' he said. 'You will fail and you know you will fail. What then? Do you propose to disturb the country by a fruitless agitation that can only result in bitter feeling and perhaps rebellion? Or will you accept the situation and devote your talents and influence toward securing the successful working of Confederation and help build a great nation in British North America?' And so, Dr. Tupper planted a seed, which Prime Minister Macdonald would water, grow to fruition, and harvest, eventually bringing me into his federal cabinet in 1868."

"Did you have any success whatsoever with the British politicians and bureaucrats? Was there ever any glimmer of hope at all of repeal?"

Joe sits down as if the weight of the world had landed on him and his once powerful shoulders can no longer bear it.

"We had none. It was as though Britain was disposing of Nova Scotia into the dustbin of history and cruelly severing the imperial ties that I had defended my entire political career and held in sacred esteem. Once I had believed that the throne of England sat above the fountain of honour and justice, that the House of Lords would do justice though the heavens should fall, that a man could go to the bar of the House of Commons and obtain fair play. Now I no longer had the same point of view."

Joe's last few words are barely a whisper. I'm ashamed at having raised what was an emotionally troubling episode in his long life. He looks as demoralized and downcast as I have ever seen him as he slowly disappears, mote by mote, in front of my eyes.

CHAPTER 29

"My apologies for Joe's departure, but Confederation, both the campaign against it and its aftermath, was very hard on him. It stirs up intense emotions, which consume him."

I wheel around from packing up my laptop to see Ennis standing beside the fireplace. The adrenalin rush of his sudden arrival courses through me for a few seconds.

"And my regrets for such a shocking entrance. I felt that I must explain things left unsaid about Joe's involvement in Confederation, as so many aspersions have been cast regarding his motivations and actions in these affairs."

"It's always good to see you, Ennis. So what did you think I should know?"

"Like all great men, and I believe Joe is one of the great Nova Scotians, he is a complex person who would freely admit that he was not always certain of his own motivations other than that he trusted them and acted upon them implicitly, regardless of the cost. And while in the darkest depths of the night I sometimes worry that Joe opposed Confederation out of animus toward Dr. T-T-Tupper and to regain the centre stage in politics—for Joe loved the popular applause—I know that he is a Nova Scotia p-p-patriot who always put his country before himself."

Ennis pauses. "If Joe was an Anti-Confederate before Confederation and for a while afterward, it was out of genuine belief that his position was in the best interests of our province and out of concern for its situation in the new Dominion. Likewise, if Joe eventually came to embrace Canada, he did so out of belief that it was in the future interests of Nova Scotia."

"But it was such a stunning reversal. He campaigned so fiercely against Confederation. How did Sir John A. ever convince him to reverse his position?"

"As Joe told you, Dr. T-T-Tupper planted the seed when we were in London to lobby for repeal of the British North America Act. Joe's accurate prediction of the impact of Confederation on our province was also a factor, as tariffs on our products doubled and Nova Scotia commerce soon began to feel the effects. Joe and the Anti-Confederates were a thorn in Prime Minister Macdonald's side in P-P-Parliament. Being an extraordinarily shrewd politician, Macdonald saw an opportunity to declaw the Anties. He reached out to Joe, their leader, with an offer to discuss what could be done to alleviate Nova Scotia's economic challenges. Macdonald convinced Joe that since Nova Scotia was now part of the Dominion, the only way out of it led straight into the arms of America."

"Shrewd of Macdonald to play that card with Joe as the son of a Loyalist."

"Eventually, they agreed upon better financial terms for Nova Scotia within Confederation. Joe's negotiations resulted in the federal government wiping out Nova Scotia's one-million-dollar debt and in the transfer of $166,000 annually into our provincial coffers for ten years. These better terms added substantially to Nova Scotia's revenues, yet were no better than New Brunswick had negotiated back in 1867."

As Ennis stops speaking, a scowl slowly darkens his dour features.

"The prime minister did not stop there. Ever the clever fox, his quid p-p-p, his quid pro quo was that in exchange for getting those concessions through the House, there had to be assurance that the repeal movement would stop. And the only assurance of that was that Joe, the movement's leader, must cross the floor and join the federal cabinet. Joe initially resisted yet he was torn. An astute political man, Joe thought he understood what joining the Government and leaving the Anti-Confederates might do to his political reputation. Counterweighted against that was the financial benefit it would bring to our beloved Nova Scotia."

"No doubt Joe put Nova Scotia first, didn't he, and chose the path that led to the federal cabinet and a better deal for our province."

"Indeed. Joe returned to Ottawa in late January, and he and Macdonald went for a walk in a park near Parliament to finalize their agreement. I had accompanied Joe but trailed behind to give the two men privacy. As they headed toward the park exit, Joe suddenly stopped and exclaimed: 'What else can I do?' He promptly sat down on a nearby bench and burst into tears. I had never seen him so despondent, and all the while that devil Macdonald had his gloved hand on Joe's shoulder, trying to console him. If he were not the prime minister, I would have knocked him down where he st-st-stood. By the end of the month, Joe was sworn into cabinet as President of the Privy Council and Secretary of State for the Provinces."

"Still, a shocking political U-turn for a man renowned for standing up for his principles. In this business all you have is your personal credibility. Didn't Joe realize the storm his actions would unleash back home?"

"He anticipated a strong reaction but felt the esteem in which he was held would shield him and provide the opportunity to explain himself. Regretfully, he gravely underestimated his ability to mend broken fences. Joe was no longer the silver-tongued, bounding optimist of his glory days, and our fair province and people had changed too. When word of what Joe had done reached Halifax via the telegraph, p-p-people were outraged. The Anti-Confederates were in disbelief. Joe, who was still in Ottawa, took far too long to return home and explain his actions, which looked crass and opportunistic without the full context and rationale."

Ennis hesitates briefly and grimly shakes his head.

"By the time Joe returned, the die was cast. Public opinion had hardened against him. Old friends refused to shake his hand or meet his eye. Young men who had once tried to emulate him crossed to the other side of the road when they saw him on Barrington Street. The most vile accusations were rudely talked about behind his back but within his hearing. And everywhere the charge was that ruthless ambition had made Joe into a t-t-turncoat. Even Will Annand, a long-time friend and political ally, turned on him with a piece in the *Morning Chronicle*."

"You mean the Will Annand whose farm Joe and his family stayed on in the 1840s?"

"The very same. Will wrote in the *Chronicle*: 'Turn backward, turn backward and blush for shame, O man whom Nova Scotia has hitherto been delighted to honour, whom she raised and petted and placed high in honourable office and who has made her so bare and ungrateful a return.'"

"How terrible for Joe. They'd been so close."

"God knows Joe attempted to counter the t-t-tide of public opinion in his tried and true ways, yet few ears were open to his words. One of his finest efforts was in a speech in Windsor when, as shouts of 'traitor' and 'betrayer' rained down on him, one audience member accused him of abandoning his principles because of ambition. 'Ambitious am I?' Joe replied. 'Well gentlemen, I once had a little ambition. I was ambitious that Nova Scotia should have a free press and free responsible government. I fought for it and won it. Ambitious am I? Well gentlemen, an old man at my time of life can be supposed to have but little ambition. But, gentlemen, I have a little ambition. I am ambitious that when, in my declining years, I shall ride up and down the length of breadth of Nova Scotia, I may receive the same sympathy, confidence, and love from her sons as in days gone by I received from their sires.'"

"That's very powerful. It's Joe at his most eloquent, but did it sway the audience?"

"Not one whit. The response was virtual silence. It was one of the most crushing scenes in weeks of such scenes. All of this was extraordinarily painful for such a gregarious and social fellow as Joe. You could see him shrink, inch by inch, under the never-ending onslaught. To be s-s-spurned by his fellow Nova Scotians, after all their battles together, broke his lion's heart."

"I feel terrible for dredging all this up, Ennis. I had no real idea of the personal cost he paid."

"And he had more of the bill yet to pay, for by the winter of 1869 he had to go back and face the people of Hants to seek re-election to Parliament, now as a cabinet minister. Joe's old enemies were now at his side, while old friends were allied against him. Yet, Joe persevered. He knew no other way. It was a bleak, cold winter. Still Joe, who was sixty-four years old and subject to wicked colds and bronchitis, threw himself into the campaign as before, only now all his magnificent strength and vigour were gone. Susan Ann and I had recommended that he quit the campaign for a brief respite, but he would have none of it."

"That must've been hard for you and Susan Ann to accept. Now that I've met Joe, I have no doubt that it would be impossible to convince him to quit anything once he set his mind to it."

"P-P-Precisely. One night we were at a political debate in an old, unheated drill hall in Welsford, and Joe was so exhausted and his back so sore that he wrapped himself in borrowed overcoats and laid down at the back of the stage to rest and gain his strength while others spoke. When it was his turn, he got up, brushed off his long grey coat, and seeing the sympathy in a few faces somehow managed to capture some of the magic of a time gone by in his oratory. Joe's courage moved some in that crowd to hang their heads in shame for having judged him so harshly. He overcame their antipathy and his opponent through sheer force of will. Afterward, Joe collapsed and had to be helped to a nearby farmhouse where he recuperated from a case of bronchitis for more than a week before returning home. It was this final electoral victory that sealed his death. His health was never the same again."

Tears are streaming down Ennis's plump cheeks and into his beard. I move to hug and comfort Joe's confidant only to helplessly grasp empty air.

CHAPTER 30

We were on the home stretch of a long spring sitting of the Legislature, and the budget, which came down in late March, was about to be passed when our Government got rocked by another scandal. Like the Upper Middlewood school controversy, it's of our own making and could've been avoided. Unlike the last one, it involves the premier.

Nova Scotia has an aging transportation infrastructure. Old bridges and roads that serve fewer and fewer people. Built to support a rural population of another era that has melted away, headed out west or to Halifax to look for work. We're left with rusting bridges on cracking secondary roads. Sometimes the locals have the option of faster, better maintained routes nearby that avoid this old infrastructure altogether while adding only minutes to their travels.

Some of these bridges, like the Devon River Bridge in the premier's district of Colchester North, have a handful of users a day. Built in 1920, it failed its recent inspection and had to be temporarily closed. The Infrastructure Department found it couldn't be safely repaired and recommended permanent closure. A replacement was estimated at $8 million or more to service a couple of dozen crossings per day, and officials decided against it.

The premier thought otherwise. The Infrastructure Department suddenly found a replacement for the Devon River Bridge on their capital priorities list for the upcoming year. Enter Opposition leader Danny Gillis who raised the issue based on a leaked email between the head of Infrastructure's bridge division and her boss, which questioned the decision.

"I'm curious to know why the premier and his Minister of Infrastructure didn't listen to the advice of the department's bridge expert who stressed that the limited traffic using the bridge—in the range of twenty crossings per day —didn't justify an expenditure of $8 million to replace it?"

The premier replied, "Unlike the Opposition leader, our Government works to ensure rural Nova Scotians have the infrastructure they need, and we deliver it as efficiently and quickly as possible. And unlike the Opposition leader, we won't turn our backs on the fine families who live on the Devon River Road. And we certainly won't endanger their health and safety."

"No, Premier, our party will not turn its back on rural Nova Scotians, but neither will we spend their money foolishly. And no, we won't abandon or endanger the families who live on Devon River Road. The *six* families that live on the less connected side of that bridge, I might add. My final question to the premier is this: has he read the email from Emergency Health Services to that same bridge official that said that while the bridge's closure would add three kilometres to the drive of any ambulance servicing those families, another road option that doesn't use that bridge is actually a quicker route to the nearest hospital?"

The stern face of Sir Charles Tupper glares down from his portrait on the wall behind Gillis, adding his weight to the calls of "shame" and heckling from the Opposition side aimed at the premier.

"Mr. Speaker, our Government remains committed to providing rural Nova Scotians with the infrastructure they need, as quickly and efficiently as possible. Unlike the Official Opposition leader who would strand rural Nova Scotians with poor and crumbling services."

Our Government is once again hemorrhaging from a self-inflicted wound. There have been days of media stories and social media coverage. The latest twist on the story, spun by an Opposition media release, is that one of the families living on Devon River Road has contributed $1,000 or more annually to our party's election fundraising efforts for the past decade.

Halifax-based cabinet ministers and Government MLAs are getting pelted by email after email and a Twitter storm criticizing the rural bias of this government. As usual, the tweets aimed at my female colleagues and me are particularly crude and personal. Probably the most damning media was a column by Pam Carvery in the *Chronicle* with the clever headline: "A Bridge Too Far."

"By greenlighting construction of a replacement for the Devon River Bridge, in the premier's Colchester North district," Carvery wrote, "this Government has again shown itself to be running an old-fashioned gravy train. This bridge and the new Upper Middlewood school are only the latest examples in a long, sad list. Perhaps for Nova Scotia voters, replacing the Devon River Bridge will prove to be a bridge too far."

The newspaper added salt to the wound with a cartoon depicting the premier in an old-fashioned train engineer's cap driving an engine pulling tankers marked "gravy" along a track with a fearful Nova Scotia taxpayer tied to the rails. The cartoonist added a villain's handlebar mustache to the premier's normally clean-shaven face. The premier has a collection of political cartoons hanging on the wall of his office, but I don't expect he'll be adding a copy of this one.

After that, our Government went into overdrive to finish the spring session and to get the four-days a week Question Period shut down. Three days of noon to midnight sittings got all the necessary legislative work completed, but it wasn't pretty. The only positive thing lately has been my EA Mackenzie who's been helping our Antigonish backbencher with the application to get a $100,000 grant from Municipal Affairs to help build a community hall in Stewartville. The tiny community has been doing bingos, bake sales, and ticket drives for years to raise money for the hall, and if the grant is approved, it will finally get done.

"If our Government can do this it will be huge," she told me the other day, her face beaming. "It's near where I grew up, so I know the difference it'll make."

Mackenzie has become as invaluable in helping me with my ministerial duties as Nada is at my constituency office. She prioritizes my work, screens tricky calls, and liaises with the PO to ensure our department's efforts are a good fit with government priorities.

I need a break from politics, which is why I'm meeting Summer for brunch at one of her favourite North End Halifax hipster places serving Asian noodles and Japanese beer.

"Curran, you look like shit. Politics is killing you. You gotta rethink this gig. If you want to stay in politics, go be the mayor or something. He's stepping down, isn't he? His gig has got to be more fun than yours."

"I know, this session ended roughly. It's been a grind. You probably heard about how it went off the rails at the end, right?"

"Something about a bridge? I heard something, I don't remember what."

This is why I love Summer. Time with her is usually the perfect anecdote to politics, and this afternoon is no different. She reminds me that despite the bridge scandal being a multi-day story, not everyone outside the political-media-business bubble in downtown Halifax follows politics all that closely. I settle into my Kirin beer and thick rice noodles.

"You know what you and Robbie the Robot need? You need a holiday. Away from Zoey. She could handle it and you know your mom and dad would be happy to look after her. Even the Robot's parents might fly in to spend time with Zoey. You could go somewhere fun and exotic like a beach in Belize or Curaçao or somewhere crazy like Iceland or New Zealand."

"Didn't you go to Curaçao with Emily, or was it the new one, Jill? Sometimes I get the order of your girlfriends confused."

"It was Emily and it was awesome. Great sun, great food, fabulous sex, but not my point, Curran. My point is you need a break."

"You're on to something. Zoey's too young to bring with us, and we couldn't stay away from her for more than a week, so that definitely takes New Zealand off the list. Robbie has always wanted to go back to London. It's nice and close. A week there, a week anywhere together, would be awesome."

"Oh my God, only you and Robbie would think of going to rainy, boring London for a vacation. Hang on, you could see the Victoria and Albert Museum. That would be pretty cool. Promise you'll take a holiday."

"Definitely, if Robbie can get the time off. Hey, speaking of Zoey, she's playing the cutest game these days. She has this little desk and she sets her toy cash register on it and pretends it's a laptop and sits her stuffies around her on the floor and gives them orders. I asked what she was doing and she said, 'I'm playing office, Mommy.' Isn't that funny?"

"She's certainly you and the Robot's kid, no doubt about it."

"Uh, Summer, there's something else I've been meaning to tell you."

I pause and look around carefully to make sure no one is sitting close enough to overhear.

"What's up? Jesus, you're scaring me. You didn't get some weird diagnosis or something, did you? Wait, are you pregnant?"

"No, sorry, it's hard for me to say this. I haven't told anyone. Not even Robbie. I know that you'll understand. It's hard to put into words, but I've seen a ghost at Province House. Not just once or twice, repeatedly for a number of months. And I've talked to him."

"What are you sayin'?"

"It seems ridiculous when I say it out loud, but last fall I saw a ghost and he began to talk to me. Then I started talking to him. Well actually, him and eventually his dead friend too."

"You're kidding me, right?"

"Honest to God. I'm only telling you because I need to tell someone. It's been bottled up inside me for like six or seven months. I knew you'd listen and wouldn't think I've gone off the deep end like Robbie would."

"I can't believe that Ms. Straight Arrow is chatting up ghosts. That's amazing!"

"Shush. I'm not looking to get any attention about this."

"And do this ghost and his ghost buddy or ghost chick have names?"

"This is the other part you won't believe. It's Joe Howe."

"You mean the guy we learned about in school? That Joe Howe?"

"Yeah, that Joe Howe. Apparently, he's been hanging at Province House since he died in the early 1870s, and in all that time he's only been able to connect with one live person —and that's me."

"That's awesome. Wow. Your dad would be super impressed. Isn't he the big Joe Howe fan? So, who's the other ghost?"

"He's Joe's aide from back in the day, a guy named Ennis Douglas. Apparently he was a well-known Halifax journalist in the mid-1800s."

"Never heard of the dude. What do you and Howe talk about?"

"Politics and political history, mostly. And a lot about his career."

"Oh my God, Curran, only you could make talking with a ghost sound boring. So, when do I get to meet him?"

"Uh, never, Summer. That's not how this works. I'm not setting up a dating service to connect living people with ghosts or doing ghost walks or anything."

"Okay, okay, I was only asking. That is so crazy. I mean, yeah, way back in the day I thought I saw the ghost of Anna Leonowens at art school. But even I admit that I was doing a lot of drugs in those days, so who knows what I really saw. Either way, I didn't sit down and have a chit-chat with her. So, what does your ghost pal look like?"

"He looks like a faded copy of the statue outside Province House, only older. Joe is very pale. He materializes out of thin air, kind of like people materialize when they've been transported on *Star Trek*. I can feel his presence when he's about to appear, like I can feel Ennis's presence, only each feels different."

"You are one lucky chick. That is so awesome."

"Yeah, it's pretty amazing."

For a moment after I drop Summer off, my mind is at peace. Sharing the secret that I've kept to myself for months is a relief, though the guilt of not telling Robbie remains. I hope the day will come that I can tell him.

CHAPTER 31

Robbie and I had an amazing week in London, staying in the Chelsea district, off Kings Road, in a small bachelor flat we found on Airbnb. Seven days of leafy walks, holding hands, laughing, smiling, browsing bookstores, wonderful food, drinking, great sex, and awesome coffee in the morning to start it all again. We were back in sync, reminding each other why we first fell in love. I felt carefree as a university student, my mind unfurling and reopening to the possibilities that life has to offer.

Robbie looked a decade younger. He's always crazy for new experiences and has a boyish love of history. He went around with this odd smile that came out when we discovered places like Lock and Company, a hatters' shop wedged between its neighbours on St. James's Street since 1765. Lock & Co. made the bicorne hat that Admiral Lord Nelson wore during the Battle of Trafalgar and Sir Winston Churchill's trademark homburg hats during the Second World War.

Our first day we woke early and headed toward Westminster Abbey. As we walked out of the Tube station, we could hear the abbey's bells ringing. It didn't open to the public for hours, and we had planned to grab a coffee and wait. Instead, we wandered toward it only to see a warder shepherding a handful of people inside.

"Are you here for morning prayer?" he asked, as we curiously edged forward.

"Why, yes, we certainly are," Robbie said, without missing a beat.

We walked into the deserted, soaring abbey, past the eight-hundred-year-old Coronation Chair, and were ushered into a small, simple side chapel with a fresco of Christ behind the altar. We sat alone, whispering, as the bells echoed through the ancient church, each peal touching something buried deep inside me, before being joined by a few Anglican priests with plummy Oxbridge accents. After the brief service's conclusion, the minister left through a side door to an outer courtyard, letting in a breeze that seemed the very breath of God. I'm not religious, but I was that morning.

Our trip wasn't all museums, theatre, high tea, and fine dining on the terrace of The Ivy in our neighbourhood. Sometimes it was dashing out of the rain into the quaint Stanhope Arms to be greeted by the roar of patrons as Arsenal scored on the telly or biting into a traditional English pie in the Nell Gwynne Tavern, a darkly intimate pub down a narrow side alley off The Strand. We were sitting at the bar of the Nell Gwynne, two amber pints of Fuller's London Pride sweating in front of us, when Robbie said something I'll never forget.

"Erin, you're a very good politician. You're smart, great at making a connection with strangers, and your empathy is obvious and genuine. You can achieve a lot with those abilities."

"If being an MLA is something you still want, you could do it too."

"No, let me finish. I've come to realize a few things. You're better at elected politics than I would've been. And secondly, I enjoy law. Sure, the corporate work isn't always fulfilling; still, it's intellectually stimulating. I like the challenge and the firm supports a bit of pro bono work here and there. I'm good with that mix. Besides, if I got back into politics I wouldn't be able to spend as much time with Zoey. I couldn't live with that."

"Robbie, the thing is, while I like helping people and working to put good programs in place, the internal party gamesmanship and the partisan sniping in the House are starting to get me down."

"There are other places someone with your skill set and profile can practise politics. Places where there are no party politics to worry about. You originally set your sights on City Hall. Maybe it's time to start thinking about it again. And why not think big?"

"Joe, it was delightful. I'd only been there once before, on a school trip, but I wasn't old enough, or educated enough, or evolved enough to appreciate all the history and culture."

"You know, I was only a bit younger than you are now when I first visited England in 1838 with my friend, Tom Haliburton, who had been many times before. He found my excitement to see dearest England most amusing, comparing me to a schoolboy anxiously awaiting the break at the end of Michaelmas term. My enthusiasm kept building during our three-week journey on the *Tyrian* until we spied a deep blue line on the horizon that a sailor informed me was Cornwall, upon which my excitement simply overflowed. I climbed into a lifeboat and dashed off some lines of verse:

'Land of my Fathers, do I then behold

Thy noble outline rising from the sea?

Is this the Isle of which such tales are told

Home of the wise, the valiant and the free?'"

"So, what struck you most about England? What do you remember?"

"So many things and people. Tom and I were there for nearly six months; we left in the spring and returned in the fall and saw a great deal, every day, for weeks on end. The cool, ethereal wonder of St. Paul's Cathedral and Westminster Abbey where I trod through Poet's Corner with the reverence of one who has made a living with the pen but whose scribblings are nothing compared to the likes of Chaucer, Master Shakespeare, Edmund Spenser, and Dr. Johnson."

"Do you know that your friend Charles Dickens is buried in Poet's Corner too?"

"As he should be, Erin. Quite right. One day Tom and I spent a day amongst the spires of Oxford and in the dark, leathery splendour of the Bodleian Library. We also toured all the various ancient armaments stored in the rooms of the Tower of London, which has sat watch over the Thames since William the Conqueror. We even saw Henry VIII's gargantuan suit of armour with a codpiece the size of a loaf of bread. One day we went to Ascot for a day of horse racing. Tom was quite a fan of the horses. We stood for the better part of a brisk afternoon in front of young Queen Victoria's box. She was only nineteen, a pretty girl with a sweet expression on her face who seemed to have a childlike interest in the social scene swirling about her. Tom and I even attended her coronation."

"I didn't know that. You witnessed the beginning of one of the longest reigns in English history. It must have been an amazing sight."

"It was an extraordinary experience. We stood shoulder to shoulder with thousands of Londoners along St. James's Street in a good-natured, heaving mass, eager to witness the pomp of her procession from Buckingham Palace to Westminster Abbey. Shortly after half past ten, the Queen's Gold State Coach appeared, pulled by eight white horses, each led by a red-coated groom. What a sight. Gilded cherubs and Titans adorned the coach while its side panels displayed scenes painted by the Italian master Cipriani. As Her Royal Highness slowly passed, the crowd greeted her with such enthusiastic demonstrations of love, fealty, and good cheer as I had ever heard. Many a tongue bid that God bless and sustain Her Majesty. On the artfully adorned balconies of the prestigious London clubs above the street, elegantly dressed ladies waved their scarves and men doffed their hats with great reverence to Her Majesty. These shows of affection visibly affected Her Majesty. More than once she turned to the Duchess of Sutherland, who was riding in her coach, in an attempt to control the powerful emotions all this evoked, as only a proper Queen might do."

"It was probably overwhelming for her, Joe, to have that kind of adulation while only a teenager."

"Quite so. Church bells pealed across London on Her Majesty's return to Buckingham Palace, with a salute from the Hyde Park guns adding to the joyous cacophony. I remember the day ended with the most fantastic fireworks I have ever witnessed, over Green Park. The coronation was an experience that was hard to capture in words, even for me who has never hesitated to try to capture anything I have observed."

"A journalist like yourself, you must have loved the newspaper stands and tobacconist shops stuffed with newspapers. Every morning Robbie and I would buy three or four—the *Manchester Guardian*, or the *Times* or *Daily Telegraph* and some tabloid, the *Sun* or *Daily Mail*, and trade them back and forth over our morning coffee. There were usually a dozen or more English papers to choose from as well as the better European papers."

"A dozen? My word, have they dwindled so? When I first visited London, there were well over thirty London dailies to choose from, with the *Times* first and foremost. I must say my favourites on my later journeys were the new *Daily Telegraph* and a creative addition to the newspaper family called the *Illustrated London News*. Its drawings brought stories to life. In point of fact, I opened it once in the early 1860s to find myself staring at an illustration of the new Halifax Club on Hollis Street. I also seem to recall quite a lovely bookstore, crammed with novels, pamphlets, and essays. It started with an *H* and was on Piccadilly somewhere."

"Hatchards. It must've been Hatchards. It's been there for more than two hundred years. Robbie and I loved it. An amazing selection. Of course we bought too many books."

"That is it. Our trip was not only about meeting officials and seeing the various sights. Tom's fame opened the doors to many country manor houses. The creator of Sam Slick was much feted throughout our stay. Regrettably, most of those we met had read a pirated version of *The Clockmaker* published by that blaggard Richard Bentley. If I had received one-fifth of what Bentley made I would have been wealthy. Oh well, it was only money, and money never seemed attracted to me nor I to it."

The edge to his voice that built up at the mention of the publishing of *The Clockmaker* in England quickly disappears. One of Joe's most endearing qualities is his good nature and apparent inability to hold a grudge.

"Yes, Tom and I dined at many fine homes, but the food served, the wines and liquors consumed, and the quality of table conversation was no better than when I visited with Tom and his dear wife, Louisa, at his estate, Clifton, overlooking our own Windsor in Nova Scotia. I would say the same for the level of debating and speeches in the House of Commons. Their brightest stars did not hold a candle to our Archibald or Uniacke or William Young, who would have mopped the floor with their MPs."

Joe makes the last comment so convincingly that it would persuade a Victorian Englishmen, before a wide smile lightens his face.

"I must say that the reporters in the Parliamentary Press Gallery were a very intelligent set of fellows. They gave me permission to sit in the gallery whenever I came to visit. Of course, the House was sitting in its temporary location in the Lesser Hall after the fire in '34 destroyed the old House of Commons chamber, the House of Lords, and much of the old Palace of Westminster."

"We toured Parliament," I tell him. "It was magnificent. To stand in Westminster Hall, under those massive oak beams that witnessed the trials of William Wallace and Charles I, was like being part of history."

"Over the years in my various journeys to London, I saw the new House of Commons opened, the Clock Tower 'Big Ben' erected, and finally the Victoria Tower consecrated in 1860. Marvellous piece of architecture. Unfortunately, those who practise the political arts inside were not as wonderful. They sold Nova Scotia down the river during Confederation without a second's hesitation. It makes one pause and contemplate."

"The British Empire has a lot to answer for. When you think about all the horrors it inflicted on its colonies, from destroying traditional ways of life to the theft of natural resources, not to mention its racism. When I was walking in the midst of Westminster's splendour, the statues of Mahatma Ghandi and Nelson Mandela in Parliament Square were a sobering reminder of that."

"Erin, why do you attack the mother country with such vigour?"

"For its pillage of India and its enslavement of Africans. For the clearance of the Scottish Highlands, its treatment of Indigenous Peoples, and the deportation of the Acadians from our shores. The Empire's record of atrocities is long."

"I grant you that during my endless sojourn here, I have awakened from my dream of the Empire's glory to reflect on its more troubling reality. Nonetheless, England has done so much for the world as the birthplace of parliamentary democracy, the forge on which it was hammered into its glorious shape. I am still convinced that the mother country spread civilizing influence and intellectual vigour across the globe to every continent."

"You can't call Lord Cornwallis's scalp bounty on the Mi'kmaq *civilized* or the Empire allowing millions of Indians on the subcontinent to starve to death during the Great Famine of the 1870s. Although not everything left in the Empire's wake was bad, we're still dealing with the fallout of some of its evils."

"You must appreciate that I was raised a Loyalist's son with the love of the British Empire passed to me in my mother's milk. I am a man of my times, and in my era the Empire was at its pinnacle, unquestioned and unrivalled.

The pull of England's commerce, its vibrant journalism, its concert and music halls and opera, its politics, set on a world stage, were magnetic attractions to ambitious young men like Tom and myself."

Joe sadly shakes his head. "Yet, how could one throw aside one's homeland? The richness of its vast beauty. The kind and loving nature of our fellow Nova Scotians. I could not, but Tom succumbed to the siren's call and moved to England to pursue his writing career and eventually, elected politics.

'Here's a health to thee, Tom, a bright bumper we drain
To the friends that our bosoms hold dear,
As the bottle goes round, and again and again
We whisper..."we wish he was here"...."'

Joe raises an imaginary glass to his friend, a sad smile on his face, and then turns in a semicircle as if toasting other long-lost friends before he slowly disappears.

CHAPTER 32

Our polling numbers are tanking. They've been dropping since the winter, kept declining over the summer, and have fallen off a cliff since Labour Day. We're gearing up for the fall session of the Legislature with the lowest approval ratings our Government has ever seen. The polls show that if Nova Scotians were asked to vote for their favourite party today, 38 percent would choose the Official Opposition, only 28 percent would choose our party, and 15 percent said they'd vote for the Third Party. The rest were undecided.

That's bad enough for the premier, but worse is that voters say the person they most support to be the next premier is Opposition leader Danny Gillis at 40 percent, followed by the premier at 20 percent and Third Party leader Shauntay Downey at 18 percent. The rest are undecided. Gillis's numbers are double the premier's, while Shauntay has never had numbers this good. They're potentially a game changer for Shauntay, one of only a handful of African Nova Scotians ever elected as an MLA since the first in 1993.

In this era of personality politics, where parties are more about the personal brand of their leaders than about policies, a leader can't afford to poll behind their own party, because he or she starts to look like an anchor dragging the party down instead of as a magnet who attracts voters.

Adding to all that is the premier's latest gaffe, the impact of which might be longer lasting than the controversy surrounding the multimillion-dollar replacement of the Devon River Bridge in his district. He has pissed off nurses and the nurses' union, and that isn't good. Nurses are the first in a long line of health care workers whose contracts have expired and whose unions are in negotiations with the Province. We have to be careful what wage pattern these negotiations set, as the other unions won't take anything less. In the midst of these sensitive discussions, our normally careful premier snapped and said something snarky in a scrum with reporters.

"Look, our nurses are already very well paid. The average nurse in this province makes well over $72,000 per year, plus overtime. They're doing all right. Anyone who says otherwise isn't being truthful. Lots of Nova Scotians don't earn half that, and they don't have the benefits and pensions nurses have either."

That's true, still it's not good politics to say so, especially now. Our nurses are some of the worst paid in Canada, but they fair no worse in national comparisons than other Nova Scotian professionals and tradespeople given our low-wage economy. The difficulty is everyone has an aunt, sister, daughter, or son who's a nurse. Nurses also have a better reputation with the public than doctors and other health care professionals. So the premier decided to throw down against some popular people.

The nurses' union has managed to frame the negotiations as not being about money. Sure, they want a wage increase, but they say their main priorities are better benefits, improved sick leave, and additional vacation time for hard-working, exhausted nurses. The reality is labour negotiations are *always* about wages. Labour leaders and their memberships will jettison other crucial issues in favour of wage increases almost every time. Plus non-monetary issues —like benefits, sick leave, and vacation—all cost the employer money too, sometimes more than a wage increase of a few percent.

Our caucus is really freaked by the polling and knows that with a fall full of tough labour negotiations, things are only going to get worse. The premier and his staff are feeling the heat. They're testy and defensive, more against internal threats than external ones.

Enter Nathalie Amirault, whose political star continues to skyrocket. She's pretty, intelligent, well-spoken in two languages, and almost twenty years younger than the grey-haired and very tired-looking premier. She handles her files well, the business community loves her, and so do most people she meets because she's personable and bright. Plus, she has no political baggage, having only been in the game for three years.

Nathalie has been careful, publicly and privately, to show no interest in the leadership, but of course she's interested. She's an ambitious person who knows she could do the job well. She has the opportunity to be the first female premier in Nova Scotia history and the first Acadian. But the other day in a scrum her response to whether or not she supports the premier wasn't as full-throated as it might've been.

"Our party has a leader, and that's the premier, and I support the party's leader," Nathalie said.

No direct hint of disloyalty, yet hardly a ringing endorsement. And so, the press gallery and everyone in political circles has started to speculate, among themselves and aloud, in news stories, newspaper columns, and over social media, about Nathalie Amirault as premier. The King is dead, long live the Queen.

Since Nathalie and I are good friends, the premier's posse—LeBlanc, Dunc, Janet Zwicker, and others—think I'm the ringleader of her merry band of plotters. LeBlanc looks at me like a dog turd she stepped in with her best shoes. Janet stares at me with naked hatred. Dunc has this unnerving grin when he sees me. After cabinet the other day, he smiled as he brushed past and muttered something like "got somethin' that's gonna fix your wagon." It was weird.

The reality is that Doug has been working behind the scenes, firming up support for Nathalie whether she knows it or not, and I bet she does. In the past few days, I've spotted Doug lunching at the Bluenose Restaurant with some of our backbench MLAs and at Cabin Coffee quietly conferring with others. I'm staying out of it. I don't want any part in a palace coup, and Robbie agrees with me.

"Disloyalty is the biggest black mark against any party member, especially a cabinet minister. If you're disloyal to this premier, why should the next one trust you?"

If the premier goes down, I'll 100 percent support any bid Nathalie makes for the leadership. Her understanding of the critical role of our cities and larger towns in growing our economy and her compassion for the less fortunate make her an ideal potential premier.

Regardless of my current neutrality, I'm paying the price for perceived disloyalty. Suddenly my department can't get anything on the cabinet agenda or any assistance from the

Premier's Office to push difficult files along. My deputy, Margie, stormed into my office yesterday angry and confused about why all of our proposals are grinding to a standstill. I told her about the politics behind the scenes, and she frowned knowingly.

"That's too bad. I've seen this kind of thing before. It's never good. If Nova Scotians only knew how much internal party politics influences external provincial politics and screws it up, they'd be shocked. And pretty pissed off too."

Exactly.

The only good thing in the midst of all this is that Robbie helped a partner at MacKay and Macdonald win a big case. It netted the firm bucketloads of cash, so now he's back in their good books. Between his success at work and his new perspective after our summer holiday, he's a new man—or back to being the man I married. I'm happy either way.

CHAPTER 33

"There was a river of brown fur, coursing across the prairies for as far as the eye could see. I witnessed the stampeding herd of buffalo from a hill in the Dakotas. The torrent switched direction like a flock of birds wheeling one way and another, mid-flight, as it encountered large boulders or other natural impediments. Some of the shaggy beasts were as much as six feet tall and two thousand pounds. The ground shook with the rumble of their hoofs as they churned up the prairie grass, sending plumes of dust high into the pale, blue heavens."

As usual with Joe, my question has unleashed a flurry of words.

"So yes, Erin, I had the opportunity to visit the Red River Colony and saw many amazing things and talked to some fine people. Nonetheless I never had the pleasure of meeting Monsieur Riel, who by accounts was a rather unique fellow. You know, Riel was schooled in the European way, yet he led the Métis, who felt more comfortable on the open prairie hunting buffalo than reading or writing. What they could tell you about the natural world would put the finest zoologists or botanists in London to shame. From my limited experience amongst them, I found them to be a wise and kind people."

The House is set to open next Tuesday, and I've slipped into the Legislature on my usual pretext of ducking in to check my phone or laptop on this cold, rainy afternoon. I'm sitting in the Red Chamber watching rivulets of water stream down the tall windows. The gloom outside has invaded this large space and dampened its normally bright spirit. Even Joe's statue outside on the Legislature's grounds seems to hunch its shoulders against the cold drizzle.

"It was months after I had been brought into Prime Minister Macdonald's cabinet as Secretary of State for the Provinces, and one of my responsibilities was the transfer of Rupert's Land from the Hudson's Bay Company to the new Dominion."

"Rupert's Land?"

"It was much of Western Canada. We talked about it endlessly in cabinet, particularly William McDougall, our Minister of Public Works, yet none of us had ever been there. Naturally, I took it upon myself to visit and learn the situation first-hand rather than through intermediaries. I have always found that to be the most sound approach."

"Joe, you were, what, sixty-five years old by then? A trip to the Canadian West in 1869 couldn't have been an easy thing."

"It wasn't a Sunday afternoon stroll at Point Pleasant, I grant you that. Still, it was wonderfully invigorating. I set out in mid-August from Ottawa, but the trip began in earnest from St. Cloud, Minnesota, the last civilized community before this vast territory. There I met up with six Canadian businessmen, all fine young fellows, who were heading to the Red River Colony and Fort Garry in search of opportunity. Admittedly it was a rather difficult twenty-two days of travel, by horse and sometimes by foot, through a landscape that was tinder dry, flat as a board, and the colour of a camel-hair coat in some places, but as we neared the Red River, it was green, wet, and soggy from a spring and summer of flooding. It could be rough going, and as the calendar turned from September to October it grew quite cold. There was so much to see. The buffalo, the antelope, and that endless prairie sky."

"Still, no matter how invigorating all the new sights were, that kind of travel at that age must've been hard on you."

"Admittedly, I was sore at the end of the day, particularly my chest, which had been bothering me for months. Yet the conviviality of my travelling companions never failed to revive me. After our modest evening repast, we would gather around the campfire, dry buffalo dung providing the fuel, to tell stories, dance jigs, and sing songs well into the night with a flask of brandy passed around to fight off the encircling cold."

"So what happened when you finally reached Fort Garry?"

"It was anti-climactic, really. Riel and his officials were nowhere to be seen, having left to stop William McDougall, recently named Lieutenant-Governor of Rupert's Land, from crossing into the territory to begin enforcing Canada's authority. The Métis had no time for McDougall, who sent in surveyors before the colony was officially transferred to Canada. Most Métis didn't have title to their farms, only squatter's rights, so were fearful of legal surveys of any kind. The Catholic, French-speaking Métis also knew McDougall was a notoriously anti-French Protestant. Frankly, I knew from personal experience that he could be quite a disagreeable soul."

We are sitting at a table set up to host the Law Amendments Committee, an opportunity for the public to weigh in on the various pieces of new legislation that will move through the House once the Legislature is in full swing.

"I assessed all this intelligence from my few weeks at Fort Garry where I made it a point to meet with the leading men of all sides, be they Métis or the pro-Canadian faction. When I left in late October, the colony was at peace."

"So you never met with Riel even once?"

"I did not."

"Or with Lieutenant-Governor McDougall?"

"I ran into McDougall in Minnesota on my return trip home as he was en route to Fort Garry. We stopped briefly on the open prairie amidst a wind to cut your throat and quickly exchanged information. I told him that I thought the Canadians could form the basis of a government but that he should avoid doing business with one particular clique. I also told him that I hoped the Métis could be brought into this political system. I added that the Indians would likely need a treaty of some sort. Well, Riel and his companions refused McDougall entry to Rupert's Land. Shortly after, Riel created a provisional government to directly negotiate entry into Canada with the Canadian government, rather than indirectly through the Hudson's Bay Company. Riel was, in effect, the government of the territory."

Joe pauses, frustration creeping across his face.

"When I returned to Ottawa, the Official Opposition hurled numerous spurious accusations at me, suggesting that my visit had somehow stirred up insurrection amongst the Métis. One impudent fellow even accused me of having drunk champagne with Riel while I was there. I was so outraged, I still remember my response: 'I never saw Riel in all my life, and I never drank champagne either with him or with anybody at Red River. In fact, I do not believe that there was a bottle of champagne in the Territory that was fit to drink.'"

"So the only federal politician with the guts to go out west and independently investigate the situation ends up being attacked for his initiative."

"Precisely. Of course, none of my protestations stopped George Brown and his Toronto *Globe* from blaming the Red River disaster on our government and on myself in particular. The Liberal press in Nova Scotia picked up the *Globe*'s theme, suggesting that I had made much mischief in Red River and that my actions had amounted to treachery. Eventually, like all political brouhahas, this one subsided too. At least it did for the remainder of my lifetime, as I knew it would, and as wily Prime Minister Macdonald counselled. 'When fortune empties her chamber pot on your head, Joe, smile and say, we are going to have a summer shower.'"

"It's a great line. Every politician would get it."

"I must confess that while the trip was boyish good fun, it caused the ruination of my health. I was no longer able to rally from my setbacks like in days of old when I prided myself on my iron constitution. Afterward, my constitution was made of porcelain, with each setback taking another chip out of it until it broke entirely in 1873."

"The trip must've been very draining. Hey Joe, before I forget, I printed off some pictures of my daughter and husband for you to see. Here's one of the two of them at the Seaport Farmer's Market and another by Griffin's Pond in the Public Gardens. Zoey calls it the Ducky's Pond."

"Oh my, your daughter is all blonde curls. What a

precious delight. And that little smile. How wonderful it would be to play on the floor with her. And your husband, a fine-looking young man. He seems familiar."

"Robbie was an executive assistant with our government in the early years. You would've seen him around here."

"Quite so, quite so. You are blessed, Erin."

It might be the kindest and most perceptive thing Joe has said to me.

CHAPTER 34

It happened again at today's cabinet meeting. For the third time in less than a year, we cancelled a perfectly good program put in place by the Official Opposition when they were in power. Not because the public didn't like the program or it wasn't working or cost-effective. Simply because it wasn't part of our platform, part of our brand. It was implemented by the Opposition, so it smells of their time in office.

New governments take power and focus on new priorities and drop the former government's priorities and programs like hot potatoes. The program we killed provided microgrants to young entrepreneurs to help start businesses. Sure, it needed tweaks and was certainly more philosophically attuned to the Opposition than to our party, but it was working.

At the end of most workdays lately, Margie stops by for a chat. I've come to enjoy these sessions. I like her company and she's teaching me how government really works. She can tell I'm upset when she walks in and probably figures it has to do with cabinet, but even a deputy minister doesn't know what's on the full cabinet agenda.

"So we killed the Entrepreneurial Microgrant Program. It was working well. Plenty of uptake, especially in Halifax and the university towns, and the small business community liked it. Still, we ditched it because it wasn't the right political colour."

"That's not unusual. Every government I've worked for over the last thirty years has done it. Some more than others. New governments often waste their first couple of years disrupting things, supposedly to improve them. It's too bad. Some good work gets lost, and the bureaucracy can end up wasting a lot of time trying to reinvent the wheel. Worse, sometimes departments aren't asked to replace good programs that were filling a genuine need."

Margie is usually very matter-of-fact about these things, but as I get to know her, I see that this foolishness weighs on her. At some point it will speed her retirement. She pauses in a way that I've come to know is quickly followed by moments of unvarnished truth.

"Frankly, none of the parties does a great job of developing policy. It's easy to throw something together in Opposition when you don't have the responsibility of power or access to all the information for sound decision making. All the parties have grand plans to change programs or create new ones. They like to come up with something that sounds dynamic and differentiates them from the other parties. Some of the political platforms we see trotted out during elections are downright scary to us old policy hands—either undoable, wrong-headed, or recycled previous failures. Nevertheless, the public service has to find a way to make them work or at least make them palatable. I'm not saying that public servants have all the answers either, because we don't. Still, if a government's new policies or programs go sideways, they never hesitate to blame it on the bureaucracy for poor implementation, as opposed to admitting they made a bad decision."

Margie's pale complexion is reddening to the colour of her hair as she gathers steam.

"What's worse is that increasingly we see-saw from one approach to its exact opposite when governments change, whether it's how to grow tourism, support agriculture, or enhance economic development. Once we change direction from going north, as one government wanted, to heading south as the new one wants, we're right back where we started and no further ahead despite years of work and millions of dollars in investment."

"We'd all be better off if the political parties could agree on common approaches to the big-ticket issues like the economy, health care, education, and culture and agree to only squabble about the timing and level of funding."

"I couldn't agree more. The adversarial approach is challenging with two different parties in play to govern Nova Scotia, let alone three. The back-and-forth policy swings leave us spinning our wheels."

"I don't see why we can't keep the Opposition stuff that works, put a new wrapper on it, and claim we improved it. The folks in the Premier's Office get so fixated on the party platforms, ours and the other parties. They think Nova Scotians walk around with them in their back pockets for comparison. Hell, most of our MLAs can't name what was in our last election platform, let alone what was in the Official Opposition's platform."

"I'm probably talking out of turn, but it goes well beyond programs. I'm a big Red Sox fan, and to use a baseball analogy, it's like when the parties are designing their election platforms, they swing for the fences, hoping for home runs, instead of trying to hit a lot of good, crisp singles. And so the platform planks are more strident than they should be, promising outlandishly positive outcomes on the issues of the day rather than modest improvements. So, instead of promising tweaks to how government is organized, to modernize it or update it, they promise wholesale changes, creating one department and dismantling another, or combining several departments. Sometimes there's some kind of philosophy behind it, but often the changes are the idea of the latest whiz kids in the PO who only care about the party being seen to offer something new and different."

"I know that's what our platform felt like when I took a close look before my by-election campaign."

"Sure, sometimes the mandate or structure of a department is wrong and it needs a wholesale change. But government departments and agencies aren't only structure. They're people too. And often as not, changing a handful of key people will do more than wholesale structural changes, which cause uncertainty and stall momentum."

Margie pauses for a moment, an odd little smile on her face.

"Some of the deputy ministers call it 'department roulette.' Each party has a way they think government should be structured. As a result, some units of government flit back and forth between various departments at the whim of our new political masters. In the past fifteen years public servants responsible for economic development have been in at least three departments, tourism has moved from one department to another to being its own agency. Our food inspectors have been part of three different departments and are back where they first started."

"All that change has to have an impact."

"Of course. These units are staffed by human beings. Each time they move, the unit loses momentum while they deal with new deputies and new ministers and get used to the different ways each department operates. As importantly, senior public servants, tired of the endless cycle of change, retire early, robbing us of invaluable, and not always replaceable, experience."

"You should write a book, Margie, or teach a grad course at Dalhousie. As for me, I'm getting fed up with adversarial politics. Surely we all want what's best for our province, even though we might not always agree on what that is. Still, I'd rather disagree about stuff that matters than about what political colour a program is wrapped in."

"Changing the subject, Erin, why is young Mackenzie so glum? She looks like she lost her best friend."

"She's been helping our Antigonish backbencher apply for a grant to help build a community hall near her home community. Just when it looked like Municipal Affairs was going to approve it, the Premier's Office swooped in and grabbed the $100,000 for a Cape Breton minister's pet project, even though it clearly didn't qualify for the grant. Apparently, LeBlanc intervened and said the Antigonish MLA lost the money because years ago, he didn't back the premier's play for party leader and the Cape Bretoner did. It was a rude awakening for poor Mackenzie. Kind of knocked the wind out of her."

Margie shakes her head in disgust.

"Christ, that was more than a decade ago. LeBlanc and the premier have long memories."

"Hey, Margie, given the way this week is going, are you up for a quick drink at The Triangle before we head home?"

"You know, I think they just might have a glass of Redbreast Irish Whiskey over there with my name on it."

CHAPTER 35

We're a few weeks into the fall sitting of the House and I haven't talked to Joe since it began. The premier's posse is freezing me out as Nathalie's alleged co-conspirator in the potential coup. Oddly, they stay clear of Nathalie, perhaps fearful of confronting her directly in case she wins. While I haven't lifted a finger to support her, Doug and former cabinet minister Grace Smith are among those who are lobbying for the premier's ouster and for Nathalie to take the leadership of the party. I could sure use some advice.

The House is done for the day and so I sit waiting in the Veterans Room as the fall light streaming through the windows begins to fade, darkening the room's normally warm hues. The hint of cigar smoke and a sudden chill tell me it's not Joe who comes to see me today.

"Apologies, Erin, Joe is feeling a bit off as of late. S-Sometimes the resumption of the Legislature affects him so. Why, I have no idea, as at least it gives us something to observe, although watching politics for as long as we have certainly does wear on one."

"I don't mean to look disappointed, it's just I'm in a difficult position and thought Joe might be able to offer some advice. You know, internal party stuff, the worst kind of politics there is. But I'm sorry, you might have advice for me too."

"No, Joe is your man. While I served him in many political capacities, it was never my forte but rather something I did reluctantly, out of loyalty. Has your situation been exacerbated by the recent unfortunate demise of Bob Stirling, the former cabinet minister?"

"Not exactly, although Bob's passing has destabilized our party. He was a big backer of the premier whose support in cabinet and caucus gets smaller with every drop in our polling numbers."

"Joe is best for advice on this matter; nonetheless your colleague's death reminds me of one subject you and I have not talked about before, and that is Joe's last few months alive. For some reason, I feel now is the right time for this conversation."

"It's always great to chat, even if what you're going to tell me will be sad."

Ennis takes a deep breath. "Joe's final days on this earth were quite sad, yet they also revealed the depth of feeling Nova Scotians had for him after it seemed they had turned their backs on him forever over Confederation. Even his new political allies in Ottawa seemed tired of Joe and eager to shove him out of cabinet as the bitterly cold winter of 1873 progressed. As much as I detest Prime Minister Macdonald, I grant that he alone stood in Joe's corner, not wanting to embarrass an old man near the end of his days in power. While the prime minister did not always see eye to eye with Joe, he told me once that 'there are more seminal ideas in that man's head—all of them important—than in any other man's with whose history I am familiar.'"

"And how was Joe feeling by then? Had he recovered from his exhausting trip to the Red River Colony?"

"He had not. His old, deep well of strength and vitality was gone. The slightest cold, a modest cough, would set him back for weeks. He was a sh-sh-sh, he was a sh-shell of himself, although his spirits were good and his mind was still strong, or pretty strong. Certainly strong enough."

The eyes of the pudgy, middle-aged fellow before me are welling up with tears, the jaw under his beard stiffening. It's as though he is re-girding himself to defend the old lion who once ruled but now faces challenges from lesser foes snapping at his heels from every side.

"In May of 1873, the prime minister found an honourable solution. Joe would replace General Sir Charles Hastings Doyle as Lieutenant-Governor of Nova Scotia when he stepped down. I t-t-travelled with Joe and Susan Ann from Ottawa to Halifax, and by the time we arrived Joe was ashen-faced and trembling. The small crowd that gathered to welcome him home were shocked by how old and feeble he had become. We had a devil of a time getting him up Government House's curved staircase to his bedroom. Later that night one of Joe's relatives came by for a brief visit. He asked Joe what his father, John, the old Loyalist, would have thought of seeing a son sitting as Lieutenant-Governor. 'It would have pleased the old man. I have had a long fight for it and have stormed the castle at last. Now that I have it, what does it all amount to? I shall be here but a few days, and instead of playing governor, I feel like saying what Wolsey said to the Abbot of Leicester:

"An old man, broken with the storm of State
Is come to lay his weary bones among ye;

Give him a little earth for charity.'"

"A few days later, a long-time follower called on Joe at Government House. The old men drew near, and as hand touched hand, the two heads bowed together, and without a word they kissed softly as young children would."

"How long was Joe Lieutenant-Governor before he died?"

"He was sworn in on May 10, 1873, standing as tall and strongly as he was able, and died at Government House on June 1, less than three weeks later, at the age of sixty-eight. I last saw him on the eve before he passed. He had been in intense pain for a couple of days, unable to lie down and find a bit of sleep. I felt horribly, as only days before I had taken him on a rather long carriage ride, twenty miles over rough roads to Deer's Inn in P-P-Preston. We had taken a few previous carriage rides that week, and he felt they were quite recuperative. I wasn't certain we should press on all the way to Preston, but Joe was insistent. It was a beautiful day and it seemed like he couldn't get enough of the outside and sunshine as one does who has walked and ridden across the length and breadth of our great province. Nonetheless, I should have put my foot down and t-t-turned the carriage around. That last morning of his life he alternated between walking the floor of his study and sitting in a chair, with Susan Ann and his son William anxiously watching him. She convinced him to try sleeping in a bed. He collapsed on the way and died ten minutes later, shortly after half past four in the morning."

Ennis stops to gather himself, tears glistening in his eyes.

"If only I had t-t-turned that carriage around."

It's one thing to read about Joe's death in a dusty history book but another to hear it from the mouth of a dear friend. His death nearly 150 years ago pulls at me more than my

Grandpa Chisholm's passing. I know Joe more intimately than I ever knew that distant man from Antigonish.

"There's nothing you could have done, Ennis. It was his time. And for someone like Joe, an active man who loved the outdoors, that last carriage ride probably meant all the world to him."

"I hope you are right. In all this time, we have never talked of it as I am too embarrassed to raise the subject, although I have described his funeral to him numerous times over the years. Certainly, it pleases his vanity to hear of the outpouring of love and genuine affection that came following his death. More than that, it reaffirms to him that the bond he always felt with the people of Nova Scotia had not broken. It had been stretched and tested but held firm."

"So how did people react to his passing?"

"The news flew through Halifax like a cold spring wind, into every nook and cranny. Flags were immediately lowered to half-mast at Government House, the provincial and city buildings, at the Citadel, on Her Majesty's Ship *Royal Alfred*, and on most of the merchant vessels anchored in Halifax Harbour from around the world. It must have quickly reached out beyond the city, for by afternoon I spied a well-known but simple farmer from outside of town looking down distraughtly at the ground as I walked past his wagon. 'Is it Howe?' I asked him. 'Yes, it's Howe,' he said, before his tears began falling like rain on the paving s-s-stones. I was told that is how many of our fellow Nova Scotians reacted, from Yarmouth to Inverness, on wharves, in fields, at country stores, and on lonely roads. I myself witnessed it for two days at Government House where people from every walk of life and of every age came to pay their respects to Joe as he lay in his open casket."

"Given Joe's long political career and his prominence, I imagine his funeral was a big affair."

"The service itself was very simple, as Joe was always a somewhat s-s-skeptical Christian. Only a short service at Government House attended by relatives and close friends, officiated by Rev. J. K. Smith, a Presbyterian minister, as that was Susan Ann's persuasion. The funeral procession, however, was a state event. A solemn-looking hearse followed by Joe's family and close friends, all dressed in black. Around them officers of Her Majesty's Army in their scarlet uniforms, as well as officers of the Navy in their dark blue uniforms. As the funeral cortège began, the minute guns on Citadel Hill fired a salute. The route of the procession—from Government House to Morris, and South Park Street to Spring Garden Road, and thence to Camp Hill Cemetery—was lined with men of the Army, the Navy, and local volunteer forces, all in their colourful military finery. About six thousand people marched in the funeral procession, including MLAs, MPs, judges of the Nova Scotia Supreme Court, the mayor and city aldermen, officers of Her Majesty's Navy and Army, as well as members of the North British, Charitable Irish, St. George's, and Germania societies."

"It sounds majestic and quite fitting, given everything that Joe had done for this province."

"My former newspaper colleagues guessed that about twenty thousand people came out to watch the procession. For such a large crowd, it was eerily silent, as though a giant had fallen, someone whose like they knew they would never see again. After all that, we lowered Joe, the most passionately alive fellow ever born, into the cold, lifeless ground of Camp Hill and walked away. To me it was as though the sun had set and been replaced by cold and unending night.

After living so long in the warmth of Joe's fire, I didn't quite know what to do with myself. As a lifelong bachelor, I had no more reason to my days. Thank goodness it was only seventeen years before I p-passed away and was reunited with him in this half-life to provide whatever limited assistance I have been able to offer. I feel you ought to know how Joe's story ended, Erin, for it reaffirmed everything about the way he lived his life."

A FEW NIGHTS later as Robbie gently snores beside me in bed, I open my laptop and go online to read some of the newspaper coverage of Joe's death and excerpts about his last days in biographies.

A contemporary of his, George Edward Fenerty, noted one telling detail about Joe. "And then, he died poor. This implies more than can be written—for with all the opportunities he had for enriching himself, as other Nova Scotians have done, Mr. Howe would despoil a friend rather than touch unhallowed coin belonging to the State. *Howe died poor*. Let this be placed as a memento over the entrance door to the vault which covers his dust."

The *Evening Express* offered this tribute to Joe, whom it described as "our greatest man": "He touched you with a tender word and you softened—even if you were an opponent. He tickled you with a humorous story—and you laughed even though you came to be angry. He flashed before you some daring smile and you felt dazzled—even though your critical taste disapproved. He flung in at random some miraculously happy quotation from some rich treasure-house of English literature—and you could not help admiring the culture of the man, even though the next moment he would offend you with a vulgarism."

"No British North American approached him in breadth of statesmanlike views," the *Halifax Morning Chronicle* intoned. "Many have grown sad with the thought that the foremost man of British America was not Canada's first prime minister. The Tuppers and Macdonalds forced themselves to the front—the old man lagged behind—because his new associates lacked generosity, and the weight of years had paralyzed his strength."

The *Chronicle*'s tribute to Joe concluded: "On Sunday morning he yielded up his spirit. The grey head that all men knew, that was carried erect to the last, is low enough now. The busy, tireless hand that performed so much labour as printer, journalist, politician, statesman, minister, is powerless. The eloquent tongue is still. The eyes that sparkled with the light of humour and the fire of genius are lustreless. And the ears that for forty years or more had been so often filled with the plaudits of thousands will soon be filled with dust."

It's like reading the obituaries of Nelson Mandela, John F. Kennedy, Terry Fox, or Eleanor Roosevelt. Lives fully lived that profoundly affected others. It makes me wonder about my own modest contribution on this earth.

Ennis once told me a story about a simple country fellow who had come to meet his idol.

"He walked into Joe's office to see Joe standing at his desk, engaged in writing. Our country friend soon felt himself at ease in the presence of the Nova Scotia icon. Joe said he was glad to see him and talked with him as freely as though they had been lifelong companions, and soon our friend thought Joe was not only the greatest man in the world, but the most agreeable that ever lived since Adam.

Joe then invited the man to dine with him, which was not uncommon for Joe to do even with comparative strangers. Eventually the gentleman had to leave for home and said his goodbyes. I ran into him on the street and asked him what he thought of Joe after spending the day with him. 'Think of him?' was the reply. 'There is no room to think at all. He is the most wonderful man I ever saw. When I entered his office, he seemed like a very ordinary mortal, about five feet high. I had not been there more than half an hour when he seemed like a man eight feet—but before I left, to my astonishment, his head touched the ceiling—twelve feet high.'"

CHAPTER 36

And then it happened, as Joe had been trying to prepare me for. Out of thin air, and outside the regular process, a request to fund a sports and recreation facility in Dunc's district landed on my desk.

Our department has a program with a limited budget to support modest construction and renovation projects for sports and rec facilities. It requires joint funding from either the federal or municipal government to qualify, preferably both. It provides a maximum of $500,000, but normally we approve projects in the quarter-million-dollar range. As it's October, we've already committed our money for this year.

Enter the Premier's Office. LeBlanc called Margie and told her that Health Promotion had to fund a project in Dunc's hometown for $1.5 million, triple the maximum that the program provides.

Margie argued that the town council hadn't applied for the funding and wouldn't qualify if it did. She added that the town didn't plan to contribute one cent to build the facility and that the project seemed wildly ambitious for such a small community. It fell on deaf ears.

"Deputy, I don't want any bureaucratic foot dragging. Find the money somewhere in your department's existing budget. I want this gift wrapped and tied up with a bow so Dunc can make a big announcement in the next few weeks. Make this happen. Do I make myself clear?" LeBlanc said, then hung up.

"Erin, I can find the money, although it won't be easy. Still, it's going to look bad. We turned down far better proposals from a few other communities after we ran out of funding. And they were asking for less money. What am I going to tell them? Besides, that town not only doesn't have the money to help build this project, it won't have the money to operate it either. Ask our colleagues at Municipal Affairs. So who will Dunc lean on to help with the operating costs when the town comes up short? You can guess the answer."

Sure, I've had to sign off on a few sketchy approvals in my limited time as a minister. A grant here or there that went to one of our districts when it could easily have gone to an Opposition district. I've tried to ensure I only do that when the sole thing that separates the quality of the two competing applications is politics. This is different.

Since I joined cabinet, Joe has warned me that in every cabinet minister's career they will face some decisions that fundamentally challenge their beliefs and values. He's a big fan of the classics and often refers to Roman history.

"As the great Julius Caesar once did, and as I did with Confederation, you too will one day face your Rubicon and must decide whether or not to cross the river that separates you from one destiny or another, irrevocably changing your fate. It may seem an odd thing to say, but it is less important to know which path is best than to discern which decisions will define your life and career and which will turn out to be regular and run-of-the-mill."

I tried to reason with the Premier's Office. LeBlanc wouldn't take my calls or stop when I tried to get her attention after cabinet. I finally managed to corner one of her underlings after a meeting.

"I know the PO wants to make Dunc's project happen. And there's no question the town lacks good sports infrastructure. Of course, part of the reason is because it has no municipal tax base. If my department announces this, there are three communities with solid projects we turned down who will immediately call my office and yours. And two of them are in districts our party holds."

"All I know, Minister, is that we've been told to make this happen, and that comes from the very top. The time for debate is over."

"There wasn't a debate. You guys handed it to us as a done deal," I said, before the Premier's Office aide shrugged her shoulders and left.

So I sit here as darkness gathers outside my office window. My choice is not as world changing as Caesar's. His decision to cross that northern Italian river with his army, against the orders of the Roman Senate, set off a civil war and altered the future of the Empire. But it's dramatic enough for me. I don't know what I'll do. I need to have a long talk with Robbie. I know what I should do. And I know where I am. I'm sitting on the banks of the Rubicon, staring across at the far shore, which marks the point of no return.

CHAPTER 37

My stress level has been soaring for the last few weeks as I grapple with the best way to turn down the outrageous request from the Premier's Office to help fund a recreation facility in Dunc's hometown.

Our whole Government is under pressure. We're well into the fall sitting and taking a pounding in Question Period over the negotiations with nurses and the other health care unions. About three hundred nurses circled the Province House block for a couple of hours today chanting "Hey hey, ho ho, the premier has got to go," blowing whistles, and waving placards despite the bitter November wind whipping along Hollis Street.

My colleagues fled as fast as they could. The Legislature staff are heading home for the weekend, and I've ducked into the library to check my phone before leaving. Robbie texts to say that I've already missed Zoey's bedtime story and she's fast asleep.

I don't know what it is about this library, maybe its walls of books or the dark wood or the tall windows, but this room's vibe of a slower and more civilized time relaxes me. A tingling sensation and the taste of copper jerk me out of my reflection, and there's Joe looking down benevolently from the top of the staircase to the second-floor book stacks.

"The premier and the Minister of Health took quite a thrashing in the House, and your fellow Government MLAs are certainly rattled by this brouhaha with the nurses. Your Government is at sixes and sevens, Erin, the cabinet wanting to stand firm against their demands while the backbenchers are inclined to acquiesce."

"Yeah, we're in a bind and the party is breaking apart over it."

"Odd that given all the exciting issues going on here lately, what with internal party dissension and these negotiations, that there seems to be fewer members of the press attending every day."

"The last few months have seen a big layoff at the *Chronicle*, and a couple of the private TV stations let people go in the spring. If you look carefully at the premier's scrum after Question Period, I bet there's 25 percent fewer journalists than when I was elected only two years ago. A lot of news outlets don't have anyone staffing the House regularly anymore."

"If the newspapers and such do not have their reporters here to cover the debates and deliberations of this body, how will our fellow Nova Scotians know what goes on? How will they learn the details, the strengths and weaknesses of the Government's policies?"

"Robbie and I worry about that. It's not good for the average person to be unaware of the actions, or lack of action, of their Government and elected representatives. Traditional journalism's ranks are so thin, and the few reporters left are so busy feeding multiple media platforms, that the news now contains mainly reports that something has occurred but without addressing the more important questions like why it happened, who made it happen, what was their motivation, and who might benefit financially."

"You and I know that the ranks of politicians include many fine fellows, and now many fine ladies, but they also include rapscallions, numbskulls, and dunderheads. A free, unfettered, and lively press is critical to democracy. To bring attention to government's successes and to warn the public of its abject failures and scandals, in equal measure. The press is always needed to keep politicians' feet to the fire."

"Absolutely. Now that I've seen the inner workings of the Premier's Office, I worry that the thinning ranks of journalists will lead to a lack of governmental vigour to ensure carefully considered decisions. I can't tell you how many times I've seen the PO or senior bureaucrats improve something solely based on a fear of it coming across as half-baked in the media. I worry that that extra effort will disappear without observant reporters."

"Admittedly, sometimes the power of the press is no more than that of a small, barking dog, but even so it at least alerts the public to lurking troubles."

"Exactly. As the labour leader Mother Jones always said, 'the job of a newspaper is to comfort the afflicted and afflict the comfortable.'"

"A bit radical for my tastes, yet with a grain of truth. The ruling compact must always be kept on their toes so that they do not forget their less fortunate fellow man."

"Unfortunately, Joe, traditional media—the press in particular, but TV and radio too—is taking a financial beating, and their influence is waning. And my fellow politicians aren't lifting a finger to help the media industry, an institution so critical to democracy."

"No doubt, Erin, democracy and the press are hand in glove. Even once I left the newspaper business, I always respected what the fellows had to say, even if I didn't always agree with their positions. At the very least I respected their right to say it and the necessity of them saying it."

"The longer I'm in politics, the more I realize how few of my colleagues are true democrats who believe in the important role the media play. Most politicians and their aides are partisans. They're not democrats. Their opinion on the quality of stories and journalists is based solely on how glowing or negative they perceive the coverage to be. Some politicians relish the decline of the traditional media because they view them as the enemy or, at best, as a needless middleman between themselves and the public."

"A horribly repugnant and short-sighted view of the important role of the men, and women, of the press."

"And if anyone in the general public is worried about a lack of government transparency now, wait until there aren't any media around to push the issue, and see how quickly government lip service to transparency fades. Sometimes I wonder why I'm still in this racket. It doesn't seem like I'm able to make much difference. My ability to change anything, to see that the right thing is done, is so small."

"'Nobody makes a greater mistake than he who does nothing because he could only do a little.' A great man once said that, I no longer recall who, but I believe they are words to live by. True, as a member of a cabinet within a government party and as an elected representative of a larger legislative body, you cannot do a lot on your own, but you can certainly do a little. And the *little* you have accomplished so far, Erin, has done far more good than you know."

"Thanks, Joe, sometimes this place brings me down a

bit. Right now, I'm facing pressure to approve funding for a project in Dunc's district that should never get the green light. Only the fear of the media exposing its sketchiness might keep the Premier's Office from making it happen. I'm losing sleep because I can't square doing what they want with what I know I should do."

"Erin, after reflection you will no doubt choose the right course. As a politician one must be creative and flexible, yet in the end one must stand by one's principals."

"I figured that's what you'd say. I just really needed to hear you say it."

"I am happy if I have been able to provide a word of counsel, for I don't know how much longer I might be here."

"What do you mean?"

"My senses are as alert as birds before a storm. Much as I once felt on the eve of a major journey or the first few times I was alone with my dearest Susie. Frankly, it is the feeling I had in the instant before my parting from this mortal coil."

"Joe, do you think...."

A stirring from the doorway behind the librarian's desk draws my attention away from Joe. It's Dunc, lowering a hand holding an iPhone.

"I don't know who in the hell you're talking to on your phone or what reporter you just ratted us out to, but that was government business you were talking about, and that's going to get you kicked out of cabinet. When I show this video to folks in the Premier's Office, it'll be the end of your political career, darling. Give my regards to your friend Nathalie."

Dunc brushes past me with an ugly leer, waving his cell-phone at me, and scuttles out of the library. I turn back to look for Joe, but he's disappeared—and so has my political future.

CHAPTER 38

"Of course I believe you. You're my wife."

Robbie gives me a long hug that helps right my tilting world. A great weight has been lifted off. Keeping this secret from him has bothered me far more than I'd realized.

"I never told you," he says as he releases me from his embrace, "but Dad swore that our cottage was haunted by the ghost of an old woman settler. From the style of her clothes, he figured she might date back to the founding families that carved out farms from the forest around our lake in Ontario about two hundred years ago. He saw her a dozen or more times over twenty years. A few minutes here and there, either sitting in the kitchen or in an old rocking chair in the living room. She didn't say or do anything, only looked at him sadly. And then she quit appearing."

"Your dad talked about seeing a ghost? That's hard to believe. It doesn't seem like your dad."

"It doesn't, but Grandma Morrison had the same kind of experiences with ghosts and spirits and so did her mother. Dad talked about it matter-of-factly, as though it was something passed on in the family genes, like brown eyes or red hair."

"I'm sorry, Robbie. I didn't know how to tell you. I was worried you might just dismiss it. I didn't think you'd react like this."

"You should've trusted me. Still, I get why you thought I'd react weirdly. The main thing now is what are you going to do? Dunc thinks he has you on video spilling cabinet secrets to a reporter. That asshole will go for the jugular. He's a vicious bastard and he thinks he's protecting his boss. Plus, he won't want the good times to stop. Nathalie will throw his ass out of cabinet if she takes over."

"He's got me, Robbie. There's no way I can fight this thing in public. I can't explain my way around the video he has if he actually knows how to work his phone. Who would believe me other than you? It'll look like I'm breaking cabinet confidentiality. I don't expect Joe shows up on the video, at least not clearly, or can be heard, if you believe all those ghost-hunter shows on TV."

"Whatever you decide, Erin, I'm behind you 100 percent."

MONDAYS ARE NORMALLY quiet in the Legislature when it's in session. There's no Question Period and we sit later in the afternoon to accommodate MLAs returning from weekends in their districts. The place has a relaxed, lazy feel with little or no political rancour. Despite that, I've been worried sick since I arrived, repeatedly checking Twitter and other social media accounts on my phone, fearful that Dunc may have already posted the video. I expect to be scrummed by the media any minute. Robbie insists Dunc will wait until tomorrow when more media will be around to ensure its full impact. He's out to sink me in the hope that anything that embarrasses me will embarrass Nathalie.

Committee of the Whole is scheduled for a few bills, and I'm on House duty. Cabinet ministers get to skip as much of the bill debates as possible to give them time for their ministerial duties, but we all have to take a turn to ensure our party maintains superior numbers in the chamber in case a vote comes up. Given his busy schedule, the premier rarely attends these sessions, and he's not here this afternoon.

Up for debate are amendments to the Fisheries Loan Board Act. Only a handful of MLAs are interested—the fisheries minister, the Official Opposition and Third Party fisheries critics, and a few others who represent fishing communities. All the rest are checking their cellphones, working on correspondence, reading newspapers, or quietly chatting with seatmates. I ask to be recognized by the Deputy Speaker, who is sitting in the Speaker's Chair to oversee debate.

"The chair recognizes the Honourable Member for Fairview–Clayton Park."

"Thank you, Madam Speaker, I am honoured to join debate on this piece of legislation. You know, it's still as thrilling to speak in this Legislature as it was the first time I did nearly two years ago when I was first elected to represent the people of Fairview–Clayton Park."

Only a few of the twenty MLAs in the House are paying attention. As I glance toward the Speaker, I see the portrait of Joe in his elder years, to her left. It gives me courage to do what I've come to do.

"That's why it's with some sadness that I must announce that I will be leaving this House and provincial politics, effective immediately. Although it has been an honour to serve and a pleasure to be your colleague, I feel I must resign."

The first eyes that pick up and look at me aren't the MLAs sitting on the floor of the House only metres from me, but the handful of cabinet ministers' EAs who sit upstairs in the public gallery. They're the political antennae of the party, and they're twitching.

"I say 'resign' because I feel I can no longer support the direction of the Government."

It's slowly dawning on the Government MLAs and the Opposition across the floor that something unusual is happening. Conversations halt and people put down what they're reading to listen. Dunc looks up from playing with his phone. Even the Deputy Speaker has been roused in her comfortable throne and is watching warily.

"I can't support a Government that isn't honest and transparent with Nova Scotians, and in particular with the urban voters of Halifax who make up more than one-third of our province."

"Does the Honourable Member have something to add to debate regarding amendments to the Fisheries Loan Board Act? That is what is at debate."

"I do, Madam Speaker. The proposed changes to the Fisheries Loan Board are the latest example of the kind of advantages that flow to rural Nova Scotia that are not offered to urban residents and, in this case, small, urban businesses. We live in a province that lives in the past and supports the industries of the past. Where political power supports our rural population at the expense of our cities. Madam Speaker, we live in a province that has aging roads and bridges and schools in rural communities that have dwindling populations. Yet we continue to fund expensive replacements while growing parts of Halifax are forced to make do with portable classrooms for jam-packed schools, gridlocked roads, and underfunded public transit."

I glance to my left and see Doug look at me quizzically, cellphone in hand, as he completes a text, probably to Nathalie. I didn't mean to take either of them by surprise, but it's in Nathalie's best interests that I neutralize Dunc's attempt to smear me, and ultimately her, by stepping down as soon as possible. It's called getting ahead of the news cycle.

"Madam Speaker, this Government needs to be transparent about the advantages offered to rural Nova Scotia through arrangements such as this Loan Board and a variety of programs. It needs to be transparent to urban voters that they are subsidizing this largesse for rural Nova Scotians. Perhaps the voters of Halifax would support this approach, but they need to be informed that it's taking place."

I look up to the public gallery and am shocked to see Joe and Ennis nodding and smiling encouragement.

"By God Joe, she is giving them what for, is she not?"

"She is doing an excellent job, Ennis. A fine woman and an honourable politician. It has been one of my greatest pleasures to make her acquaintance. Her departure will be an immense loss to this House, yet who knows where her political future lies. I am certain that it will be bright. You know, I am surprised to say this, but after nearly 150 years, I shall miss looking down on the debates below."

"Madam Speaker, we allow rural municipalities to get away with not pulling their weight. They get financial breaks and aren't always asked to provide their share of funding for infrastructure that requires joint funding. Instead the province pays its share and then quietly steps in and pays the municipality's share too."

A couple of reporters have arrived in the press gallery above us and are scribbling furiously in their notebooks. Some major players from the Premier's Office are hustling into the public gallery too, including his head of communications. They are staring down at the Deputy Speaker and trying to grab her attention to shut me down.

I stop for a quick sip of water and look around to see every face on the floor of the Legislature staring back at me intently.

"Finally, Madam Speaker, Nova Scotia prides itself on being the birthplace of responsible government and having the first such government in the British Empire. We achieved this through the tireless efforts of Reformers like Joe Howe, Herbert Huntington, and James Boyle Uniacke who acted on the popular will of the people. Their work enabled elected politicians to become the executive that ran this province rather than the governor's unelected Executive Council. What would these great Reformers say today if they saw unelected Premier's Office staff effectively running our government? Would the premier's staff look much different to them than the governor's appointed Executive Council members of the past, which they fought so hard to replace? I wonder—"

"I believe the Honourable Member is out of order, Madam Speaker," Janet Zwicker says, quickly rising from her seat to urge the Speaker to end my little tirade.

"Yes, the Honourable Member for Fairview–Clayton Park is out of order."

"Madam Speaker, I would protest your ruling, but perhaps it's time for me to either sit down or leave. But before I go, I urge my fellow members to remember why you're here."

"Order, please. Order," I hear the Speaker insist.

"You weren't elected to be a string puppet controlled by a premier or party leaders. You were elected to represent the hopes and aspirations, the values and beliefs of your communities. Thank you and goodbye."

I walk out the doors of the chamber—past a glaring Janet Zwicker, a grinning Danny Gillis, and a confused Dunc McDonald—toward a handful of reporters and a couple of TV cameras waiting in the foyer, outside the Legislative Library.

"Minister Curran, can we have a word with you?" a young reporter from the *Chronicle* asks.

I stop as TV camera lights turn on, broadcast microphones thrust forward, and reporters crowd around me, their cellphones out to record my comments. Outside this circle, an outer ring of political aides from all the parties forms to hear and record the exchange.

"So, Minister, can we get you to say what you said in there? Why are you resigning from cabinet and from the Government?"

"I said pretty much everything I had to say in the chamber. I can no longer support the Government. It's too focused on the interests of rural Nova Scotia at the expense of urban Nova Scotia. The future of this province is Halifax and a few other growing urban areas. Government needs to be honest with Nova Scotians about that."

LeBlanc has made her way over from the Premier's Office to a few feet behind the circle of political aides. If looks could kill I'd be on the floor with a chalk outline around my prone figure.

"Look, I'm not saying Government should write off rural Nova Scotia. It's the heart and soul of our province. The spirit of Nova Scotia lives in our rural areas. And some rural parts of the province contribute greatly to our economy. But Government has a responsibility to be honest with urban taxpayers so that they know they foot much of the bill for our current focus on rural Nova Scotia, that's all."

"Can you get into specifics, some examples?"

"I am leaving cabinet and the Government, but I feel honour bound not to discuss specifics that I learned at the cabinet table. All I can really say is that I have observed this approach, not only in my time in cabinet, but also as a Government MLA."

"Are you on the outs with the premier or any of his cabinet? Is that why you're resigning?"

"No, this isn't a personal thing, it's a matter of differing points of view. In fact, I didn't tell either the premier or any of my fellow MLAs that I was resigning. It seemed the right thing to do when you no longer agree with the decisions being taken."

"Are you doing this to oppose the premier's leadership or to support someone else's leadership aspirations?"

"If that was my motivation, I wouldn't have resigned. I would've stayed in Government. I'm not resigning to protest anyone or to support someone, I'm doing it because I no longer believe in the direction of the Government. That doesn't mean the direction can't change, but I won't be part of it."

"Does too much power rest in the Premier's Office?"

"You know, every few years Nova Scotians undertake an important democratic responsibility and vote to choose their MLA, which in turn determines who will govern our province. Surely, we don't go through all that effort to elect MLAs to Province House, to the people's house, only to have the premier and a handful of unelected staff make all the major decisions. So the short answer is, yes. The Premier's

Office has too much power over elected cabinet ministers and elected MLAs."

"Is this the last of Erin Curran in the political arena? Will we see you in provincial politics again, or for that matter in federal or municipal politics?"

"I'm not certain party politics is for me. Too many decisions are driven solely by politics and party one-upmanship as opposed to what's in the best interests of Nova Scotians. And I think our politics has become too adversarial. The level of partisanship in this House needs to be seriously toned down. All three parties should work together for the best interests of Nova Scotia. To paraphrase Joe Howe, demagogues of all parties like to find fault with everything, propose nothing practical, and oppose whatever is suggested. They like to misrepresent and defame. Joe said the goal of honest and rational politicians ought to be to understand each other, to deal frankly and fairly with everyone, and to give fellow members credit for a desire to get to the truth."

On the edge of the scrum I notice that Robbie has come over from work to support me. He smiles and gives me a discreet thumbs-up within sight of LeBlanc, who flashes him a sour look.

"One last thing. Democracy is too important to be left to politicians and political parties to control, especially governing parties. Nova Scotians need to be vigilant to ensure fair processes. Maybe the public needs a say in regulating party nominations. To set spending limits for nomination contests and to standardize the timing of nominating meetings, that kind of thing, to ensure party insiders don't gain unfair advantage. After all, those nominations decide which candidates voters have the choice to elect. Without fairer nominations is it any wonder we end up endlessly electing middle-aged white men?"

"So, Minister, you're not necessarily excluding a run at municipal politics. You sounded like a city councillor in there. Would you consider running for council next fall or even for mayor? The mayor has said he's not reoffering."

"I'm only thirty-seven so I can't say you'll never see me in elected politics again. I'm not actively considering municipal politics, but I'm not dismissing it either. I've thought a lot about urban planning, climate change and sustainability, about housing and public transit, and about how to build a healthy, liveable, and inclusive city. I'm intrigued by the possibilities. Halifax Regional Municipality has never had a female mayor. I think it's time, don't you?"

As the scrum ends, I thrust a hand into my blazer pocket and discover something tucked inside. I pull out the calling card of the Honourable Joseph Howe, Lieutenant-Governor of Nova Scotia. On the back, written in a quick hand: *Love all, trust a few, do wrong to none. – Master Shakespeare.*

Robbie pushes through the crowd and whispers congratulations in my ear. I need to get out of here so grab his hand and pull him down the staircase toward the first-floor exit. I come to an abrupt stop on the landing when I see Joe and Ennis below, walking across the checkerboard floor of the main lobby. They hesitate before first one and then the other plunges through the closed double doors leading to Hollis Street, like divers being swallowed by dark water.

"What the hell? They haven't been able to leave here for nearly 150 years. Where are they going? Wait, Robbie, let's get the car. We need to get somewhere fast. For some reason I think I know where those two are heading."

CHAPTER 39

"Where are you going?"

"I am quite convinced that I shall be able to pass through the solid main doors of Province House and walk out onto Hollis Street."

"Why that is absurd, Joe. We have not been able to leave this p-p-place in nearly 150 years. Why should this day be any different, despite its significance in the life of our poor Erin? The attempt will only disappoint you. Joe?"

"I am through the door. You must step outside. It is magnificent. God's teeth, the air, the breeze, trees full of birds singing their wonderfully optimistic hearts out. Absolutely delightful."

"Oh my. You are right. It is wonderful to be out of doors. And look at that sky. Glorious. Good, God, what was that thing that flew past on the street like a lightning bolt?

"I believe it to be a horseless coach of some kind. Extraordinary speed. Here is another, and another. Who would dare to cross the street? It would take a fellow in fine form to make that dash safely. Ennis, do not feel alarmed, but it appears my feet are not resting upon these steps and neither are yours. We are floating inches above the granite and being drawn southward. How extraordinary."

"Look, Joe. I believe that statue in the middle of the green is you. I would recognize that silhouette anywhere. The sculptor has certainly captured you in full oratorical s-s-splendour, right hand stretched out for emphasis, a speech crumpled in your left. I have seen the same pose from you on stages in Pictou, Yarmouth, Lunenburg, and one hundred other places."

"You think so? He has been kind and gilded the lily. I am not certain that I was ever so handsome. My father and brother John certainly, but not this squat, large-headed fellow with the big nose."

"Note the inscription on the plaque: 'Journalist, orator, statesman, prophet, patriot, Briton.' Born...such and such... died...well, we know that...etcetera, etcetera. 'I wish to live and die a British subject but not a Briton only in name; give me, give my country the blessed privilege of her constitution and new laws. Let us be content with nothing less.' Why Joe, you continue to be revered in our native land."

"It is quite touching to know that one is remembered for having done his all for Nova Scotia. It warms the heart, or at least where a beating heart should be. I have this feeling that you and I are about to leave this lovely garden bound for elsewhere. My gracious, we are ten feet off the ground, higher than the spiked iron fence protecting Province House. It is as though we are climbing a grand, airy stair-case. Ennis, what stands over there where old St. Matthew's Church rested before that fire in the 1850s?"

"A sign out front says that tower of brackish-coloured glass is the Joseph Howe Building. The accolades continue to rain upon you. Why your namesake and these other massive glass t-t-towers all about us put even the tall and foreboding T-Tower of London to shame. Wait. Where are you going?"

"We are but two leaves floating down a river as it wends its way toward the sea. Some other hand guides our journey. Come along. I hardly know where we go. Nothing appears familiar to me in a city I could once walk blindfolded. Wait. Up ahead. There is the copper-clad steeple of St. Paul's Church, anchoring Barrington Street as it has always done, even before my time. The dry sermons inside never appealed to me, yet it is such a lovely church. Watch yourself, you almost floated into the branches of that tree. It is a most disconcerting mode of travel. Ah, the Grand Parade still stretches beyond St. Paul's, but I have no idea what that sandstone building is at the north end. Could it be a new Dalhousie College?"

"Do I espy a plaque below that says it is City Hall? Where might Dalhousie College have gone? Surely, it continues to exist somewhere in this city?"

"Look, Ennis, to your left, up on Argyle Street. An old friend, the National School. I wonder, do boys and girls continue to receive education for free within? It seems much expanded in size."

"A canopy over the windows indicates it is The Five Fishermen Restaurant and Grill. The building feeds stomachs now, not minds. Another friend is ahead, the Old Town Clock. Why it gleams as though newly built and freshly polished."

"And it appears to keep the measure of time for Haligonians as it has always done, with Citadel Hill squatting behind, as ancient as a Buddha. How many soldiers checked its face before reporting for duty? Which lovers did its hands part at the close of an evening? More than you and I could count. This floating height we are attaining makes one quite breathless. I have never suffered from vertigo, but this makes me appreciate its frightful power."

"It's delightful! It reminds me of the view from Mr. Green's air balloon above Vauxhall Gardens on that trip to London. Do you recall the extraordinary views of the north bank of the mighty Thames from high above the Gardens? From our height here, one can appreciate the star shape of the Citadel fortress. Exquisite geometry."

"Goodness, look eastward. Why, it is my much beloved McNabs Island where Susie and I nestled together under stars and sky so very long ago. Oh, the warm memories it stirs. How peculiar not to see any sailing vessels gliding past in the harbour. I would love to linger a while and enjoy this sainted view, yet I feel we are once again being pulled along. Could that tree-lined field next to Citadel Hill be the Commons? As a young boy I watched the Regiment drill and parade there on Sundays. Dressed in their finest, all the young maids watching for their beaus. Hang on. Can you not smell the delicious tang of salt water? It is the Northwest Arm."

"Joe, I recognize nothing. It is as though the rain has erased a chalk drawing of our Halifax. Yet by God that is Deadman's Island if I am not mistaken, and to the right of it must be your dearest p-p-playmate, Melville Island."

"So it is. How often I stared across the glassy waters and gazed upon Melville's hidden charms. I can see nothing of my venerated father's humble cottage or of the outer buildings that were once my playground. It saddens me to see no vestige of that wonderful refuge. Even so, the Arm retains all of its lustrous and silken beauty."

"Joe, we are ascending. My word, up into the very clouds themselves and hurtling over trees, ponds, bogs, and open fields. Above slivers of road slashed through forests and rock to link towns where quiet villages once slept. And now coming down, down, landing light as feathers, but where?"

"Bless my soul, we are in a vineyard heavy with ripe grapes. Have we been blown off course to old France or Germany, perhaps somewhere along the Rhine? Wait, there is mystical Blomidon looming ahead and across that inlet of the Minas Basin are the glorious Acadian dykelands of Grand Pré. There can be no doubt. We are in the most fertile place in Nova Scotia, the Annapolis Valley. It has changed so and yet its fecundity is the same. One can feel it flowing up through one's boots."

"Off we go, even faster and higher than before. How exciting. Where to next, I wonder?"

"Below is the sandstone of Convocation Hall at King's College, so no doubt it is to Windsor. And look. I see Tom's estate spread before us. Clifton House, altered perhaps, yet unmistakeable, even from this great height. Oh, the wonderful summer afternoons and winter evenings I spent with Tom and his charming wife, Louisa. Sharing a convivial hour or two over a few glasses of good French brandy. There are few men whose politics I disagreed with more profoundly, yet whose amenable disagreement I relished more than that of Tom Haliburton. Oh, I sense we are leaving. On and on we go. Will we never stop again?"

"At last. We are out of the clouds and have come to rest, I believe, at the foot of the Bedford Basin, amidst all of these criss-crossing train tracks. Joe, your dream of ever expanding railways has come to fruition."

"Indeed, it is wonderful to see this road of iron stretching toward the capital of Nova Scotia commerce with its linkage to the ocean and seagoing vessels. See there, next to the basin's edge, the Duke of Kent's old music room, sparkling beside the darkening waters of the Basin with a dazzling coat of white paint. Why I never saw it look so fine in my lifetime. When I was a young man, it and other parts of the Wentworth estate had fallen into disrepair. It was not nearly so gay a retreat as in Prince Edward's day."

"And still we are pushed forward. Will our travels never cease?"

"Ennis, I feel we may be coming to the end of our winged flight. We are landing, but this time in a cemetery, Camp Hill Cemetery. And look, standing under that elm are Erin and Robbie. Why does she not approach? She is giving a sad little wave as though I am heading up the gangplank for a long journey."

"Joe, I must leave you here, for I believe I know why this is our destination and why Erin came to say goodbye. I must say that it has been my honour to walk beside you, to offer what modest assistance I might, through much of your life and now in this after t-t-time. Our journey together is at an end, to my most profound regret. Goodbye. I believe you might want to head in that direction, toward that granite obelisk."

"Is that where my mortal remains lie? Within the cool bosom of Nova Scotia soil? Ennis? Ennis? Sleep well, noble friend. Am I to soldier on alone without peace? Wait, what stirs beside my grave? Bless my soul. Susie, is it you holding out your loving arms? Why you are as a blushing young maiden on McNabs under the eternal celestial sky. My dearest, my beloved."

ACKNOWLEDGMENTS

I have had in mind to write a historical novel about Joe Howe, Nova Scotia's most famous journalist and politician, for the last decade, but was squeamish about putting my modern mind in the head of a real, historical person.

In 2015, the idea of combining elements of Nova Scotia history and politics with today's provincial political scene came to me and *Joe Howe's Ghost* was born. I have made every effort to ensure Howe's views on events during his lifetime -- his famous libel trial, the fight for responsible government and his battle against Confederation – reflect historical fact. Joe's thoughts on what he has seen in 150 years of haunting the hallways of Province House, however, are solely my conjecture.

Many people helped polish my manuscript along the way. My thanks first and foremost to my wife, Karen Shewbridge. In all my writing she has always been my toughest editor, but also my most passionate supporter. Her belief in this project was absolute. The feedback and input of our daughter, Kier, and our son, Cale, helped immensely to flesh out the modern story line and to develop Erin Curran's character. My daughter-in-law Amy LeBouthillier provided artful feedback on the book cover's design.

A big thank you to my editor, Marianne Ward, who helped me meld the story of the past with the story of the present and to find the proper balance between them. I am forever in your debt for your wise counsel and careful, scrupulous eye.

Also, thanks to Nancy Cassidy for a final copy edit, for editing my book cover, for helping to format the manuscript and for her advice on independent publishing.

A huge thank you to my illustrator Ivan Zanchetta, for capturing the spirit of my text in one powerful image.

I must pay tribute to a number of authors and historians for helping me to understand Howe, the history of Halifax, Nova Scotia politics and Province House. Chief among them: J. Murray Beck, J.A. Roy, J. W. Longley, Kay Hill, George Edward Fenerty, Rev. G.M. Grant, William Lawson Grant, Brian Cuthbertson, Paul Bennett, Joan M. Payzant, David McDonald and, of course, Joe Howe himself.

Through the course of my writing, I have been guided by the words of Irish novelist and playwright Samuel Beckett: "Ever tried. Ever failed. No matter. Try again. Fail again. Fail better."

I have thought long and hard about politics for 40 years in my careers as a journalist and as a government communicator. *Joe Howe's Ghost* is the culmination of those thoughts. I look forward to my next writing project and to failing better.

ABOUT THE AUTHOR

Bretton Loney is a novelist and non-fiction writer who has published two books that were nominated for Whistler Independent Book Awards: a biography, *Rebel With A Cause: The Doc Nikaido Story* in 2015 and in 2018 his first novel, *The Last Hockey Player.*

His short stories have appeared in various Canadian short story anthologies and literary journals, including the short story collection *Everything Is So Political.* In 2019 his story, "The Coulee Song", appeared in *The Group of Seven Reimagined*, a collection of very short stories inspired by the artists' paintings.

Loney was a journalist for more than 20 years in Nova Scotia and Newfoundland and worked in government communications for more than 15 years. He lives in Halifax with his wife, Karen Shewbridge. For more information, please see www.brettonloney.com

Made in the USA
Middletown, DE
13 August 2022

71196602R10136